# GOOD GIRL NEXT DOOR

## THE JETTY BEACH SERIES BOOK 6

CLAIRE KINGSLEY

Always Have LLC

Copyright © 2017 Claire Kingsley

All rights reserved.

No part of this book may be reproduced in any form or by any electronic or mechanical means, including information storage and retrieval systems, without written permission from the author, except for the use of brief quotations in a book review.

This is a work of fiction. Any names, characters, places, or incidents are products of the author's imagination and used in a fictitious manner. Any resemblance to actual people, places, or events is purely coincidental or fictionalized.

Cover by Kari March Designs

Edited by Serenity Editing Services

Published by Always Have, LLC

Previously published as Could Be the One: A Back to Jetty Beach Romance

ISBN: 9781797053592

www.clairekingsleybooks.com

❦ Created with Vellum

# ABOUT THIS BOOK

*Good Girl Next Door was previously published as Could Be the One: A Back to Jetty Beach Romance.*

**He'll teach her to be bad**

The new girl next door? She's adorable, but totally off-limits. I don't do commitment—been there, done that, got the broken heart—and sweet-as-pie Becca is too close to girlfriend material.

But she asks me to help her find her naughty side, and I'm the perfect guy for the job. She wants to take some risks and face her fears, and I have all kinds of ideas. I just need to keep my dick—and my heart—out of it.

After all, we're just two friends having fun. What could possibly go wrong?

Suddenly single, and on my own in a new town, I decide it's time to stop being so predictable. I'm tired of being the good girl. And who better to help me out of my shell than my new neighbor, Lucas?

Sure, he's sexy as sin. And as our adventures in naughtiness escalate, my lady parts are not complaining.

We agreed to stay just friends. We wouldn't let this get complicated. But Lucas is kind of amazing. And the more time we spend together, the more my heart wants things he can't give.

# 1

## BECCA

My hands tremble as the host hands me a menu. I'm trying so hard to act like I don't know what's going to happen, but I do. I *know*. The night has finally arrived. Brandon is going to propose.

I'm wearing my favorite dress—dark blue with a sweetheart neckline and an A-line skirt. Really, it's Brandon's favorite dress, but that's the point. My blond hair looks perfect, for once, and I dabbed on a little extra makeup, opting for soft pink lipstick and a little shimmer in my eyeshadow. I almost put a clip in my hair that has a white silk flower, but I changed my mind at the last minute. Maybe wearing a white flower—so much like a wedding flower—to my engagement dinner would make it too obvious that I know.

Brandon looks so nervous. I'm a bit overdressed compared to him, although he's still handsome in a dark green sweater with his shirt collar showing. In my fantasies, he's always wearing a suit when he gets down on one knee. But that's okay. I don't need every detail to be perfect.

I look up at Brandon and smile. He puts down his menu

and wipes his palms on his thighs. He keeps doing that. I'm nervous too, but it's an excited kind of nervous, all these little pings of electricity running through every nerve. We've been dating for four years, and living together for almost eight months. I've been expecting a proposal. There have been a few times I got that fluttery feeling in my tummy, like it might be coming. Last Christmas, when we were with his family. Or when we took that trip to Victoria. But he still hasn't popped the question. I've told myself he wants it to be a surprise, so a family dinner or a weekend getaway are too obvious. He must want to keep me in suspense so I don't see it coming.

Tonight, I'll act totally surprised, even though I'm onto him.

I almost told my girlfriends Madison and Juliet, but since I didn't, there's no evidence I suspect anything. They're always on my case about Brandon. They don't understand why we're not engaged yet, like there's some sort of dating time limit before you have to either take the next step or break up. There really isn't. Juliet's engagement was so out of the blue, none of us saw it coming—least of all her. But her relationship with Finn was that way from the beginning. And since Madison got married, she's been obsessed with the notion that the rest of us need to get married too.

But just because my two best friends are now married or engaged, and I've been with the same guy for four years without a ring, does *not* mean there is something inherently wrong with our relationship.

I've always assured Brandon that there's no pressure. I've made it clear I'll be happy when he does propose, and the answer will of course be *yes*. He doesn't have anything to be nervous about there. But he's skittish about marriage. I've never pressed him about his past, but I don't think he was ever serious about a woman before me. In fact, I hate to admit it, but I'm pretty sure there were a lot of women coming in and out of his bedroom before I came along.

But we've been happy together, and I've been fine with not rocking the boat. I can be patient, because I know it'll be worth it in the end.

"So, Becca." Brandon presses his lips together and runs a hand through his blond hair. "There's something I've been needing to talk to you about."

I take a careful breath so I don't seem too excited, and set my menu in front of me. "Yes?"

"Well," he says, and folds his hands together. "We've been together for quite a long time now."

I nod. "We have."

"And I think there comes a time in a relationship when we have to make decisions about the future."

My heart beats faster. "Yes, of course."

He pauses, and I wonder where he's keeping the ring. He's not wearing a jacket, so he can't produce it from an inside pocket. Maybe he gave it to the waiter, and they'll bring it out on a little plate. Or in a glass of champagne. I'm surprised he's doing it before we've ordered, but maybe he's so excited, he can't wait any longer.

"Becca..."

I lean forward, the word *yes* already on my lips.

"I think we should break up."

For a second, the words don't register.

Did he just say *break up*? My lips part and I stare at him, dumbfounded. His brow furrows, and a look of guilt passes over his features.

"Becca?"

"I'm sorry, what did you say?"

Brandon winces, and the waiter chooses this moment to

come over to take our order. I don't look up. My eyes are locked on Brandon. What the frick is even happening?

Brandon tells the waiter we need another minute and looks back at me. "I'm sorry, I guess this is kind of sudden."

"Sudden?" My chest constricts and I feel like I can't get enough air. "Sudden?"

He puts up a hand. "Okay, don't freak out."

I look at him in disbelief. Freak out? Why would he think that? I never freak out about anything. "What? No, I just... I don't understand. You're breaking up with me? Why?"

He lets out a breath. "It's not you. You're a great girl. I'm just in a place in my life where I need something else."

My stomach starts to churn and a cold sweat breaks out on my forehead. "*Something* else? Or *someone* else?" By the way Brandon winces again, I already know the answer. "There's someone else?" I put a hand to my mouth.

"Yes, but no," Brandon says. "Nothing happened with her, I swear. I've never cheated on you."

"But you *want* to cheat on me," I say, my lower lip trembling.

He opens his mouth like he's going to argue, but he looks away without saying anything.

"I thought you were going to propose tonight," I say, my voice weak. Immediately, I wish I hadn't said it. I feel so stupid.

His brow furrows again. "You thought what? Oh god, Becca."

"You never wanted to marry me," I say. "I thought you needed time, but you knew, didn't you? You knew you didn't want me forever. You knew I wasn't the one."

"I'm really sorry," he says.

My stomach turns again and there's a burning sensation

in the back of my throat. I don't understand. How could this have gone so wrong? Why didn't I see this coming?

Brandon starts talking again, but I'm not sure what he's saying. Something about *moving to the East Coast to be with her*, and *now you can find the right guy*. Does he think he's doing me a favor? My vision goes blurry, the tablecloth turning into a hazy mass of white.

"Becca?" He leans forward. "Are you okay? You don't look so good."

I shake my head slowly, my eyes on the table. I spent most of the last four years believing I was with *the one*. The guy I was going to marry.

He never felt the same way.

I suck in a breath and try to clamp a hand over my mouth, but it's too late. The contents of my stomach come racing up my throat, and before I can even think about running to the bathroom, I vomit all over the table.

And all over Brandon.

I snatch the cloth napkin and cover my mouth, my eyes wide with horror. Brandon's face is contorted with revulsion as he looks down at his soiled sweater. The people at the tables around us go quiet and stare.

I think I might die.

I get up so fast my chair falls backward, and I run out the front door.

## 2

## BECCA

*M*oving is hard.

My feet hurt, my back aches, and all I really want to do is curl up on the couch in my jammies and watch a movie. Preferably something happy.

But my new place is a disaster, and I sent everyone home. My dad insisted on hiring movers, and no matter how many times I told him I want to do this on my own, he wouldn't listen. He booked them anyway, and in the end, I'm glad he did. They moved all my stuff out of my parents' garage, hauled it the three hours to my new apartment, and unloaded it here. My friend Juliet and her fiancé Finn were here for a while to help me unpack, but I told them I have a handle on it, and they could go.

After Brandon broke up with me, I had to move out, so of course I went running home to my parents' house. I hated to do it, but Madison just got married, so I didn't want to impose on the newlyweds. And Juliet moved out to Jetty Beach to live with Finn, so that wasn't exactly convenient. But moving back in with my mom and dad was such a blow. It's bad enough that they were so eager to have me home. I guess that's better than parents who are grumpy and judgmental about it. But they act like I'm still a little girl.

They've never changed my room, so I found myself sleeping in a twin bed with a frilly pink canopy over the top. My princess bed. I got it when I was six, and oh, how I loved that bed. The framed print of Princess Aurora from Disney's *Sleeping Beauty* is still on the wall, and a hundred other reminders of my childhood are placed neatly around the room. It isn't that my childhood was bad. It was fine. My parents are nice, we lived in the same house my whole life, and I was generally happy.

But my mom and dad don't seem very interested in the idea of me actually growing up. At least, they don't like the idea of me growing up and being on my own. They insisted I live on campus my first two years of college, and paid for my room and board, because they thought I'd be safer that way. Then, when Madison, Juliet and I decided to get an apartment together, they helped us find one, so we didn't end up in a bad neighborhood. They even kicked in more for my rent, so we could afford something nicer. After college, I lived with friends for a while, and later Madison and I shared an apartment. My parents weren't totally keen on Madison—she is admittedly a little crazy—but the main thing they always insisted on was that I not live alone. After Madison got engaged, I hinted to Brandon that I needed a new place to live, and he eventually suggested I move in with him. Looking back, he was pretty hesitant about it. I should have known something was wrong, but I was too focused on playing house to see the signs. I thought if we lived together, it might speed us along to the getting-married part.

So there I was, sleeping in my childhood room, and I realized something: I've never been on my own. Not really.

I've always relied on my parents, or my friends, or my boyfriend to take care of me. I didn't mean to be that way. I never planned to be the girl who's never paid her own bills, or been responsible for the grocery shopping, or done anything close to acting like an adult. People always do things for me. My parents took care of everything until I graduated college. They said they wanted me to focus on school and didn't want me to have to worry about anything else. When I lived with Juliet and Madison, Juliet always handled the bills and things for the house. She's super organized and good at it, and also a massive control freak, so Madison and I let her. We gave her our share, and she took care of the details.

When Brandon and I moved in together, it was really *me* moving in with *him*. And he took care of everything too. At the time, I didn't think much about it. I guess I was used to it. My parents did it, my friends did it, and I slid into an easy routine of letting Brandon handle everything.

So, I decided I need to grow up. Maybe even live on my own. That thought was scary, but the more I considered it, the more I realized it's exactly what I need.

My dad tried to talk me out of it, but when he saw I wouldn't budge, he sprang into action. He found me a cute one-bedroom about two miles from their house. I couldn't really afford it, but he and my mom offered to make up the difference.

I walked around that apartment, and despite the designer finishes (quartz countertops and stainless steel appliances), it made me want to throw up again. It didn't feel like a place I could call home. It felt like a cage.

So I did something I've never really done before. I told my parents *no*.

They didn't know how to handle my sudden bout of

defiance, but for goodness sake, I'm a grown woman in my twenties. I don't need to do everything they say.

And that's when I got a little crazy.

I decided that not only do I need to live on my own, I need to get away from the place where I grew up. I've always lived in Seattle, and I sort of figured I always would. But suddenly the city felt stifling. Like there's nowhere to go where I can have any privacy. Nowhere that will let me be myself.

Almost on a whim, I declared that I was moving to Jetty Beach, a quaint little tourist town on the coast. It isn't completely random. My friend Juliet lives here now, and that's mostly why I decided on it. Starting over in a new place is all well and good, but starting over with a friend nearby is better. I won't depend on Juliet for anything. I found my own apartment, signed my own lease, and made my own arrangements. Of course, there's the thing about my dad hiring movers, but I guess I'll consider that a gift from him and not let it ding my pride that I'm not one hundred percent on my own with this move.

So here I am, sitting in a mostly-still-packed townhouse apartment, on my first night living totally by myself.

I half-heartedly try to put a few more things away, but at this point, I'm just done. I grab a slice of cold pizza out of the fridge—Finn brought over pizza for us at lunchtime when we arrived—and sit on the couch. My TV isn't hooked up yet, so I scroll through Facebook on my phone while I eat.

I'm feeling pretty proud of myself when I hear something through the shared wall. My new place is in a triplex, and I'm on one end. It's been quiet next door all day, but now I hear what sounds like a door closing. Not long after that, there's music, muted by the wall, but not much.

I've actually met my neighbor once, but it was a while

ago, when Juliet first met Finn. We were down here for her birthday and spent a Saturday night hanging out at the Irish pub Finn owns. I think Finn wanted to impress Juliet, because he invited a bunch of people to come hang out. It was fun, and I remember chatting a little with Finn's friend Lucas—who is now my neighbor. When I told Juliet I wanted to move to Jetty Beach, she gave me the lead on this place. She knew from Lucas that the last tenant had moved out.

But I have yet to see him, and I don't remember much about him anyway. I was pretty tipsy—Finn is such a good bartender—and that night is a bit of a blur.

I indulge in a second piece of pizza and flick through some Instagram posts. I hear something else through the wall, and for a second, I think maybe someone is knocking on Lucas's door.

Then I realize that's not the kind of banging I'm hearing.

Oh god.

Is he?

I listen harder, moving toward the wall, almost involuntarily. I can still hear music playing—these walls are paper thin—but I hear something else too.

The loud moan clinches it.

Yep, I can hear him having sex.

My face heats up and I know I'm blushing from the roots of my blond hair to my belly button. I'm *such* a blusher. I get red over just about anything, but listening to someone else have sex? This is mortifying.

It's not like I've never been on the other side of the wall from someone having sex before. I lived with Madison for years, and before she met her husband Eric, she was pretty free with her sexuality. I heard her with her boyfriends plenty of times. I tried not to make a thing out of it. Once, when she realized I must hear her, she apologized. But she laughed a lot while she said sorry, so I don't think it bothered her that I heard. She was laughing *at me*, knowing it made me squirm.

Now? Hearing this is making me so uncomfortable. How can he be so loud? He must know how thin the walls are. Does he just not care?

I hunker down in the cushions, pull the blanket over my lap, and search for some cute puppy YouTube videos. I need a distraction. I do not like what listening to this is doing to my insides. Dare I admit that, despite the fact that I'm horrified, I'm also feeling a little turned on?

That's so *wrong*. Isn't it?

I find another cute puppy video. This one has a kitten too. Super not sexual. I shift a little. Are my panties wet? You have *got* to be kidding me. They are.

I head upstairs and take a shower, mostly to drown out the noise. And I will not admit to what I do in the shower. No way. That's something I almost never do, and never, ever talk about.

ALL IS quiet when I wake up in the morning (thank god I don't hear morning sex coming through the wall). I head downstairs, feeling pretty proud of myself. I did it. I moved into my own place. I slept here by myself. No parents. No roommates. No boyfriend.

I'm officially a grown-up.

But this grown-up needs coffee, and I don't know where my coffee maker is. I decide to head into town to get some, and then I can start tackling the rest of this apartment.

I throw on some jeans and a sweater and head out,

slinging my purse over my shoulder. I get in my car, turn the key in the ignition, and realize I left my phone inside. I won't be gone long, so I don't really need it. But I'd rather bring it, so I hop out of my car and run up to my front door.

Just before my hand touches the doorknob, I realize what a dork I am. My keys are still in my car, and my front door is locked. I go back to my car and pull on the door handle.

Uh-oh.

I pull again, but the car door is definitely locked. I go around to the passenger side, but it's locked too.

*Oh, no.* I race around to the driver's side again and try the door, but I already know it's futile. I have a habit of locking the door from the inside when I get out, just in case the remote doesn't work. My dad taught me to do that. But this time, I left the car running when I got out, and apparently I still locked it.

I look back and forth between my apartment door and my car. I'm standing here, in the chill morning air, next to a locked car that is still running. My phone is in my apartment. My keys are in the car.

So I do what any capable adult would do. I break down in tears.

What am I going to do now? I don't know anyone nearby except Finn and Juliet, and their place isn't walking distance from here. Nothing is walking distance from here. I look up at my neighbor's door. The last thing I want to do is knock and ask him for help. Not only do I not know him, I don't want to be the weird girl who shows up at the door when his girlfriend answers in her underwear or something. How awkward.

I shuffle back up to my doorstep and try my front door

again. But of course I locked it. I always lock my door. I'm careful about that stuff.

My lower lip trembles and I sink down onto the step, a few tears sliding down my face.

I couldn't even make it twenty-four hours on my own. I'm hopeless.

3
───

# LUCAS

*I*t's kind of early for a weekend, but I'm up, and I'm out of pretty much everything, so I figure I'll run to the store. I grab my keys and head out to my car.

I'm halfway to my parking spot when I notice the car next to mine—a little red Toyota Prius—is running without anyone in it. I guess the new girl next door is warming it up. I wasn't home for most of the day yesterday. When I came back, I noticed the car, but I missed the moving truck, if there was one. I glance back at her door, and that's when I see her, sitting on the doorstep, her head in her hands.

That's weird.

"Hey, are you okay?" I ask.

She looks up and it's obvious she's been crying. Despite the fact that her cheeks are a little splotchy, she's really cute. Shoulder length blond hair, big brown eyes. Her lower lip trembles and a tear trails down her face.

I glance between her and the car a few times. She didn't...

"Oh shit, are your keys locked in your car?"

She nods.

Oh, man. That sucks balls. "And your front door is locked, too?"

She nods again.

I'm hit with a pang of sympathy for the poor girl. Although I'm not sure why she's just sitting there crying, like she's helpless. "Well, I guess you need to call a locksmith?"

She sniffs again and gestures behind her. "My phone is inside."

"Gotcha," I say. I guess this is the part where I offer to help? "Do you want me to call a locksmith for you? You can come in and wait inside my place."

Her eyebrows draw together. "No, I wouldn't want to intrude."

"It's fine."

"But isn't your, um..." She pauses for a second and looks away. "Isn't your girlfriend in there?"

"My what, now?"

"Your girlfriend. I heard... that is, it sounded like you had your girlfriend over last night."

I'm not sure what she's talking about, because I definitely don't have a girlfriend. And last night... Oh. Right. Girlfriend she was not, but I did have a girl over. "Oh, I guess I did have someone over last night, but she's not my girlfriend. And no, she's not here. She left last night."

"Oh."

"You heard, what, talking?" I ask.

Her face turns scarlet. "No. I mean, yes, that must be what I heard."

I grin at her. "Oh, I get it. Sorry."

"The walls are really thin," she says.

"I'll keep that in mind." I reach out my hand to help her to her feet. "I'm Lucas."

She takes my hand and stands. "Yeah, I'm Becca."

"So do you want to come in, or is sitting out here more your style?"

She glances at her still-running car.

"It's not like anyone can steal it," I say.

"Yeah, of course," she says. "Sure, I'll come in."

I bring her inside and notice her looking around, her eyes wide. This building used to have three units, but I took out most of the walls in two of them when I bought it. Now my side is big, and really open. There's a bedroom and bathroom upstairs, as well as a bath downstairs, but otherwise, it's all open space. My work area is set up in what used to be one of the dining rooms. I have a u-shaped desk with half a dozen computer monitors. On the other side, a couple of couches face a flat-screen TV on the wall. I took out one of the kitchens and turned it into a gaming area, with a big pool table and a few vintage arcade games.

I lead her over to one of the couches and move some things off to the side so she can sit down. She looks around like she's not sure if she wants to touch anything. My back prickles at that. Come on, my place isn't that bad. It's not even dirty; there's just a pair of jeans and a sweatshirt in her way.

She sits and I make a quick phone call to a locksmith in town. "He'll be here as soon as he can."

"Great, thank you." Her eyes dart around and she's right on the edge of the couch—clearly uncomfortable.

"You won't get a disease in here or anything," I say.

"Oh, no," she says. "Your place is nice. It's so big."

"Yeah, I combined two units when I bought the building. I like having room to stretch out."

"You own the building?" she asks.

I sit on the couch across from her. "Yep."

"How did I not know that?"

"I have a property management company deal with the rental unit you're in," I say. "I'd let you back into your place, but I don't keep a key here."

She glances over at my desk. "Is that your home office? What do you do?"

"I'm a day trader. So I work from here."

"What's a day trader?" she asks.

I shrug. "Basically I buy and sell stocks on a short term basis for quick profits."

"Wow. Sounds risky."

"It can be, but I seem to have a knack for it." I narrow my eyes at her. I know I recognize her. She's Juliet's friend, I know that much. But do I know her from somewhere else? I'm positive she's not some girl I slept with. There's no way I'd forget her if I had.

"Oh, shit," I say, recognition dawning on me. "I do know you. You were at the pub that night when Finn met Juliet."

She nods. "Yep."

"Right, you were the one who wouldn't stop talking about her perfect boyfriend," I say, laughing at the memory.

The touch of a smile I was starting to get out of her melts away in an instant, and suddenly she's crying again.

Oops.

I have a feeling I know why Becca just moved in next door to me.

"Hey," I say, feeling a little awkward. "It's okay."

"Oh my god." She sniffs hard and wipes beneath her eyes. "I can't believe I'm sitting here crying. I'm such a child."

My eyes drift down to her boobs, and *child* is definitely not what I'm thinking. "No, you're not. It's fine."

"It's just... I thought Brandon was going to propose. And then he broke up with me. Not only did he break up with me, he left me for someone else. Some fricking brunette. He moved across the country to be with her."

Okay, first of all, she's telling me things. This isn't really my area. This is more Finn's thing. She should be sitting at his bar, spilling her guts over a drink. Probably something fruity, but that's Finn's thing too. I'd have no idea what to order a girl like this. Second, she just said *fricking*, which is both hilarious and kind of adorable. Before I can stop myself, I let out a quick laugh.

Her eyes lock onto my face. "You're laughing at me?"

"No," I say, but she clearly doesn't believe me. "Not at all. It was just cute the way you said *fricking*."

"Well, Brandon is such a... a fricking jerk."

"Wow, we really need to work on your swearing."

She glares at me, and she's even cute when she does that. Everything about her is positively dripping with *adorableness*. Is that a word? Can I put *-ness* on the end of that? Whatever. It works.

"I don't need to swear to have an intelligent conversation," she says.

"No, of course not." I lean forward and put my elbows on my knees, looking her straight in the eyes. "But wouldn't it feel good to call him a fucker?"

Her cheeks color, a little flush of pink that creeps across her fair skin. And that, my friends, is my kryptonite. I start to get hard, and I'm glad I'm leaning over, because she probably can't see my crotch. I'm going to have to do some mental gymnastics to get the thought of her sweet round tits turning pink for me out of my head so I can get up without causing a scene.

But before I do, I kind of want to push her a little.

"Come on," I say, my voice gentle. "Say it once."

"Say what?"

"Brandon is a fucker."

She pinches her lips together and they move, like she's working her tongue around her mouth.

"Say it." I lick my lips and watch her think about it. "Wait, don't."

Her eyes widen with surprise. "What?"

"You've never said *fuck* before, have you?"

"What do you think I am, nine years old?"

I glance at her boobs again. "No, but you never swear, do you?"

Her eyes dart away. "No."

Oh my god. She's, like, a swearing virgin. This is magnificent. Is this girl even real? She's tiny, and blond, with chocolate brown eyes and this innocence about her that is so fucking genuine.

I kind of want to dirty her up a little.

"Okay, we're going to pop your fuck cherry, right now."

"What?" she asks, her voice going high-pitched. She leans away, like if I get too close I'll soil her.

"Yep. I want to hear you say it."

"No," she says. "I definitely can't."

"Why not?" I ask. "It's just a word. And trust me, sometimes it feels really good to say it."

"But it's so vulgar," she says.

She says that, but there's interest in her voice. She wants to be a little naughty. To take out some of her anger and hurt.

"You know, some say only unintelligent people swear, because they can't think of something better to say. But I disagree, and the research backs me on this. It takes intelligence and a good grasp of both language and social nuance to swear properly."

"So you're saying you think smart people swear?" she asks.

"Stupid people *can* swear, obviously. Smart people know how to swear *well*. And honestly, sometimes there's just no substitute for throwing out a solid *fuck*." I give emphasis to the word, letting it glide from my lips. It's like it sits there in the middle of the room between us, hovering in the air.

She opens her mouth, but closes it again.

"Come on, Becca," I say, leaning back. "Let me hear you call Brandon a fucker."

"I don't think I can."

I raise my eyebrow at her and one corner of my mouth drifts up in a half-smile. "We both know he's a fucker. He led you on, letting you believe he was going to propose, and then he left you. That's a fucker if I've ever heard of one. He deserves it."

"Well, yeah, he does."

"Good." I stare at her lips, so soft and pink. It's very difficult not to imagine those lips around my dick, but I do my best to put that thought aside. Contrary to what my friends think, I don't bang every girl I meet.

And no matter how luscious her lips are, Becca is already in my off-limits category. She's my neighbor, and as they say, I don't shit where I eat.

But this girl needs something from me that isn't my cock. She's hurt, and I'm all too familiar with the nature of this kind of pain. Seeing her grapple with it dredges up feelings I'd rather not deal with again.

What she needs is to get a little angry. To indulge in some rage toward the asshole who broke her heart.

I'm having a hard time imagining how any asshole could break *this* sweet girl's heart, but that's neither here nor there.

"Come on, Becca. Say it. Brandon is a fucker."

Something in her eyes changes. She loses the angelic doe-eyed expression, and I see a flash of anger. There's some heat behind that pale skin. Some fight in her.

I like it.

She takes a deep breath. "Brandon is a fucker." Her hand immediately goes to her mouth.

I grin at her. "That's brilliant. Say it again."

Her eyes dance and she nibbles on her bottom lip for a second before speaking. "Brandon is a fucker."

"Good. Now again, with some feeling," I say, clenching my fist. "Put some anger into it."

Her eyebrows draw together. "Brandon is *such* a fucker."

"He really is," I say. "What a douche. Go ahead, get angry."

"How the... fuck could he do that to me?" she asks, only hesitating for a second before dropping the f-bomb. "He's horrible. He's the worst. He's such an asshole."

"Good," I say, nodding. "Mix it up."

"And I'm glad I puked on him."

I laugh, and she starts laughing, and I have no idea what she's talking about, but pretty soon we're both cracking up.

"Wait, did you just say you're glad you puked on him?" I say when I can breathe again.

"Yeah," she says. "We were out to dinner, and I thought he was proposing, but instead he broke up with me. And then I threw up all over him."

I can't help but laugh again, so hard my side starts to hurt. Luckily, she laughs along with me.

"That's one of the best things I've heard in a while," I say. "I'm glad you puked on the asshole too. So, was I right? Did it feel good to say it?"

"Yeah, it did feel a little good," she says.

"Awesome."

There's a knock at the door and I get up to answer it. It's the locksmith, and Becca steps outside to talk to him. The way this guy basically breaks into her car makes me a little nervous. I wonder if he's a car prowler on the side. He's quite good at it.

Becca looks like she's ready to hug the guy, and he leaves without even charging her. I kind of can't blame him. Seeing that big smile light up her face was pretty satisfying.

She turns off her car and makes a show of bringing out her keys, holding them up and jingling them around.

"Careful with those," I say. "You won't always have me around to rescue you."

Something about the smile she gives me sends a trail of warmth through my chest.

"Well, hopefully I won't need any more rescuing."

She says goodbye and goes back into her apartment, presumably to get her phone. I head for my own car. I pull out onto the street, feeling pretty good about myself. I did my good deed for the day.

Becca might be off limits, but there's still nothing terrible about having a hot girl living next door to me. And Becca is all kinds of hot, in her oddly angelic way.

## 4

## LUCAS

My phone rings while I'm in the shower. Who's calling me? Civilized people text these days, so it must be my old man. Sure enough, I check when I get out and I have a voicemail from my dad.

I have no clue why he insists on leaving me voicemails. They always say the same thing: "Lucas, it's your father. Call me." I don't think he's ever left me a message that says anything different. I've tried to tell him that I'll see he called, and he doesn't have to leave a message if all he's going to do is tell me to call him back. But he still does. Every time.

I rake the towel over my hair a few times and wrap it around my waist. I wander over to the front window and glance outside. Becca is struggling to close her trunk with her arms full of grocery bags. I haven't seen much of her since she locked her keys in her car a few days ago. I'm not avoiding her, exactly. But I haven't gone out of my way to see her, either. She's a little too attractive. Too tempting. I should have known better when Juliet said her best friend needed a place to live. Juliet's hot—not that I'd say that in front of Finn—so I shouldn't be surprised her friend is too. I could have told Jules the apartment was already rented. Having a woman like Becca living next door is an invitation to trouble.

She slams the trunk shut and looks at her car with a self-satisfied smile. Honestly, could she be any cuter? She's like this sweet little cherub, with her bouncy blond ponytail and perky tits. And that ass. Damn, she has a great ass, and she's wearing a pair of shorts that show off every curve.

Welp, looks like jerking off is suddenly on the agenda.

It takes no time at all to get off. I start thinking about Becca, wondering if she's hiding a naughty side under that good girl exterior. Maybe she isn't hiding it. Maybe it's repressed. Fuck, that's even better. I imagine doing all sorts of dirty things to her, and I come so hard it makes my vision go dark for a second.

Shit.

Well, I guess if I'm going to live next door to a hot girl, at least she makes a fucking awesome jack-off fantasy.

I call my dad back and he wants me to come down to his store. He owns the local hardware store—it's been in the family for two generations. Unfortunately, he's always wanted me to take over for him when he retires. I worked in his store up until I went to college. I knew how to work the cash register from the time I was about ten. He pushed me hard to get a business degree, so I'd be prepared to take over for him someday. He was pissed as fuck when I switched to finance. Even more pissed when I stayed in New York and didn't move home after I graduated.

When I did eventually move home, he figured I'd step right back into his plans for me. That was the reason I almost didn't come. But my life crashed and burned pretty hard in New York, and I was ready for the slower pace of small town living. I could have moved somewhere random where I don't know anyone—and believe me, I almost did. But at the end of the day, Jetty Beach is home. It's like a completely different world from other places I've lived, and that's a lot of its appeal. I still work on East Coast time, so I'm up early—but I'm done early too. I can spend my afternoons surfing, or meeting up with friends, or even just hanging out by myself at my place. Jetty Beach is full of tourists for a lot of the year, so it's easy to meet women. So for the most part, I'm glad I moved home. Although dealing with my dad can be a pain in the ass.

I head over to his store and find him in the back. He's dressed in his usual weathered jeans and Murphy's Hardware t-shirt.

"Hey, Dad."

"Here, help me with these." He gestures to a stack of brown cardboard boxes.

I let out a breath to suppress my annoyance, and help him without complaining. He always makes me do something when I come by, under the guise of *helping*, like I'm still his employee. We move the stack of boxes from one place to another—I guess there's a point to it, but I don't know what it is.

"So, what's up, Dad?" I ask when we finish. "Did you call me down here because you needed an extra set of hands, or was there something else?"

"I heard from your mother the other day."

That gets my attention. My parents divorced when I was in college, after my dad found out my mother had been having a long-running affair. She moved to northern California and married the prick. I didn't go to the wedding. Since then, Mom and I patched things up, for the most part. I see her a couple times a year, and do my best not to punch the asshole she's married to in the teeth. But I know she and my dad don't talk very often.

"What's up with her?"

"She wanted to talk about you."

"Why did she call you to talk about me?" I ask. "She has my number."

"Don't ask me why that woman does anything," Dad says. "I guess she's worried about you, and she doesn't think you'll tell her if something is wrong."

Oh, great. Here we go. "And obviously you told her I'm fine."

"I'd be happy to tell her you're fine if that were true," he says.

"Except that it *is* true," I say. "There's literally nothing wrong with me. I think that meets the definition of *fine*."

Dad presses his lips in a thin line and turns away.

"Oh, no," I say. "We're not doing that thing where you look at me all disdainfully, but won't tell me what the fuck is wrong."

"Watch your mouth," he says.

"Fuck, Dad. Fuck."

He glares at me. "This is what I mean. You're too old to keep acting like a child."

"I'm sorry, I won't swear in front of you. But I don't think a couple f-bombs make me a child."

"You move back here, but you refuse to work for me," he says. "And even worse, you won't get a real job."

"I have a real job."

"What you do isn't a real job," he says. "Who do you work for? Who's your boss? Do you have benefits? You're basically gambling, Lucas. That's not a career."

"I work for myself, and I prefer it that way," I say. "We've been over this. I'm good at what I do. I'm not just good—I'm amazing at it. And it's hardly gambling. Yeah, it's risky, but I'm not risk averse. And I'm smarter with my money than you give me credit for."

I also make a lot more money than he realizes. I think he'd get off my back if I showed him what I have in my bank account. Multiple bank accounts. But I never go there. I'm worried it would hurt his pride too much. My dad is a hard-working man, but he's never had much. Most years, his store is in the black, and we always had what we needed, if not a lot more. But he's going to have to keep working hard until the day he retires to eke out that meager living, and if it weren't for the money I've been putting aside for him, he'd be lucky to retire when he's eighty. I'd like him to understand how successful I am, but I'm afraid it will hurt him more than it will ease his concerns about me.

"It isn't just your so-called job," he says. "You act like you're still an eighteen-year-old kid. The surfing, the girls. Don't think I'm not aware of your reputation around town when it comes to women."

"I don't have a reputation."

He quirks an eyebrow at me. "Even your mother heard."

"Heard what?"

"It's all this social media crap," he says. "Your mother has friends on, what is it, Facebook? She's friends with some people from town, one of them being Diane Miller."

Oh, great. "Angela Miller's mother?"

"That's the one," he says.

Angela Miller is the reason I no longer eat at the Porthole Inn. She's a waitress there, and I'm pretty sure she wants to murder me.

"I don't know what Diane Miller told Mom, but it's none of their business," I say.

"Why can't you just date a girl, like most men your age?" he asks. "Haven't you sowed enough wild oats?"

"I'm not sowing anything, and that's such a weird expression," I say. "I had a thing with Angela. I was honest with her from the beginning, but we wanted different things. End of story."

"I still don't understand why you didn't stay with that girl in New York," he says. "What was her name?"

"Valerie," I say through gritted teeth.

"Right, Valerie," he says.

I pinch the bridge of my nose. Valerie is not my favorite subject. "You were pissed when I stayed in New York with her. Now you're pissed that I'm not with her?"

"At least you were settled."

"I thought so too, but she had other ideas about what *settled* meant," I say. "I don't want to talk about Valerie, Dad."

"You're going to wind up getting some girl pregnant," he says. "I thought once you were done with high school, I wouldn't have to worry about that anymore."

I groan. "Dad, I'm a grown man. I haven't been a stupid teenager for a very long time. You really don't need to worry about me. I'm fine. My job is good. I'm making a good living, and I take care of myself." *And I'm going to take care of you when you're too old to work, so shut it, Dad.* "As far as dating, or whatever, I know Mom wants me to find *the one* and settle down. I have no idea why she's suddenly so obsessed with that idea. But I'm sorry to tell you, that's not me. If she's looking for a big wedding and a bunch of grandchildren, she's going to be disappointed."

My dad takes a deep breath. "All right. If she calls again, I'll tell her to quit fretting. I don't know why she's suddenly so worried about you settling down, but she is."

"My life is awesome, Dad," I say. "Seriously. I don't want

to change a thing."

He raises one eyebrow at me, like he's skeptical.

"And speaking of my awesome life..." I back away, hoping he's not going to rope me into something else. "I have to go."

"All right. Bye, son."

I breathe a sigh of relief as I get in my car. You'd think my parents would have quit trying to meddle with my life by now.

Becca's car isn't there when I get home. Before I can wonder what she's up to, she pulls up behind me and parks in her spot.

I get out of the car and grin at her. "Hey, neighbor."

She looks down at the keys in her hand before shutting her door, and I suppress a chuckle.

"Hey. How's it going?" she asks.

"Can't complain," I say. "Are you all unpacked?"

She walks around to the front of her car, holding a small shopping bag from my dad's store. That's funny. I wonder if we were just there at the same time.

"Yeah, pretty much." She holds up the bag. "I just needed a few things to hang some pictures. Although, maybe I should have asked if it's okay first?"

"Sure," I say. "Nail holes are no big deal to patch later. Need any help?"

She glances toward her front door, then back at me. "Um, no, I think I can handle it."

"You sure? I don't mind."

I have no idea why I'm pushing this, or why the smile that crosses her face makes me glad I did.

"Okay, I guess so," she says. "Come on in."

All right, part of *why* is that I'm curious what her apartment looks like.

She unlocks the door and we head inside. Her place is everything I thought it would be. No, it's *more* than I thought it would be. She has a light gray couch with pink throw pillows in the corners, and a cream-colored coffee table. Her little round dining table has two chairs painted white with turquoise legs, and there's a Mickey Mouse clock already hanging on one wall. Everything looks expensive—not a piece of Ikea furniture in sight—and it's right on the edge of being too girly for a grown woman. But not quite.

"Cute place," I say.

"Thanks," she says. "Just no going upstairs. Down here looks pretty put together, but upstairs is still a disaster."

"No worries," I say, although of course my curiosity extends to what her bedroom looks like. "So, what are you hanging?"

"This." She grabs a large framed picture that's leaning against the wall and turns it so I can see.

It's a watercolor, almost abstract, but the shape is the silhouette of a man, and a woman in a dress, facing each other.

"That's pretty."

"Thanks," she says with a big smile. "It's Sleeping Beauty, from the Disney movie. It's one of my favorites. I figure this is subtle enough that it doesn't look like I have little kid art on my wall."

She gets out the box of picture hardware from the plastic bag and eyes it for a few seconds.

"Do you have a hammer?" I ask.

"Right," she says. "I'll be right back."

She runs upstairs and comes back holding a pink plastic box with a small handle. She opens it and her eyebrows draw together. Inside are a few tools—hammer, screwdriver, crescent wrench. All with pink handles.

*Of course* her tools are pink.

"These look really stupid," she says. "My dad bought this for me so I'd have some tools. He tends to go a little overboard on the girly stuff."

I shrug and grab the hammer. "Hey, if it works, it works."

I help her hang the picture above the couch. She steps back and eyes it for a moment, then smiles at me. "That's perfect. Thank you."

"Anytime," I say. "So, dropped any more fuck bombs lately?"

Her face gets a little pink—and I get a little hard.

"I don't think so," she says.

"Need to?" I ask. "Or is everything great in Becca-land, so profanity isn't necessary."

"I think I'm good. The Brandon thing…" She waves a hand, like she's dismissing the issue. "I'm getting over it. Anyone who could do that doesn't deserve me. So…"

She trails off, but I know she's on the brink of saying it. I raise my eyebrows and smile at her.

"So, fuck him," she says.

"Yes!" I hold out my fist and she bumps it with hers. "Good girl."

I hesitate for a second. I kind of want to stay and hang out with her, but I don't want it to get weird. She glances at me like she's not sure what to do next either.

"All right, cool. Let me know if you need help with anything else." I jerk my thumb in the direction of my place. "You know where to find me."

"Thanks," she says, and her blush deepens. "I will."

We say goodbye. I head straight upstairs when I get into my apartment. That thing she does where she gets all flushed and warm-looking is killing me. I need to jerk off again.

# 5

## BECCA

Juliet's text comes at just the right time.

*Meet me at the pub? I don't have a lot of time, but I want to see you!*

I text back. *I'd love to! Be there soon.*

It's been a busy week, and I haven't seen Juliet at all. I've been unpacking and trying to get settled, which is taking forever. But I love being able to put things where I want without worrying about what my roommate or boyfriend thinks. It's very freeing.

Sleeping alone is getting easier too. I'm ashamed to admit, I was nervous about sleeping in my apartment by myself. I wondered if every little noise was going to freak me out. But it's been fine.

Knowing Lucas is right on the other side of the wall makes it easier. If something horrible did happen—like a home invasion, or a huge spider—I know I could run over there and he'd help.

However, I'm going to avoid that if at all possible. I don't need to go running to someone else every time something intimidating happens. That's what I've always done, and I'm going to stand on my own two feet, even if that means killing a spider.

Maybe. I might make an exception if the spider is really big.

I head down to Donal's Irish Pub and find Juliet sitting at the bar. Her fiancé, Finn, owns the pub, and often works as the bartender. Finn is a total sweetheart, with messy dark hair and nice eyes. The best part about him is the way he looks at Juliet, like the sun rises and sets with her.

Juliet hops off her stool to hug me. "Hey! How's the new place?"

"It's good," I say. "I still have some unpacking to do, but it's getting there."

"Awesome," she says. We both slide up onto a stool and face each other. "I'm excited to see it. I haven't come by because I didn't want to overwhelm you before you're ready for visitors. But if you need help, just ask, okay?"

"Oh, I know," I say. "I'm fine, and I'll have you guys over soon."

Finn passes me a drink. It's my favorite, a Dirty Shirley. I never have to order when I'm here. He always guesses what I want, and somehow he's always right.

"Have you met Lucas yet?" she asks. "I guess you kind of met him before, but I wasn't sure if you guys remembered each other."

I try not to cringe, thinking about the incident with my keys. At least it seems like Lucas didn't tell anyone, if Juliet hasn't heard. "Yeah, I met him a couple times this week."

Juliet leans closer and lowers her voice. "I know I gave you the lead on that apartment, but I'm worried that wasn't a good idea."

"Why? The apartment is nice."

"Yeah, it's cute. But you're living next door to Lucas."

"What's wrong with him?" I ask. "I thought he was Finn's best friend."

"He is, and he's a totally nice guy," she says. "But he's..."

"He's what?"

"Well, he's something of a man-whore."

My cheeks warm, thinking about what I heard through the wall. "Yeah, I think there was something of that nature going on my first night in the apartment."

Juliet rolls her eyes. "Of course there was. Seriously, stay far away from him. Be friendly or whatever, obviously. He's nice, and he's tons of fun to hang out with. But when it comes to women, he's trouble. He has a new girl practically every week."

"Really?"

"Yep," she says. "He doesn't really date, in the conventional sense. He just meets women, especially women who are in town visiting, sleeps with them, and sends them on their way."

"Yikes." I wonder if this means I'll be treated to a lot of nights like the first one. Although I haven't heard anything since. I shift in my seat, feeling suddenly uncomfortable. "Why do guys do that?"

Juliet shrugs. "Because they can? Who knows. I just don't want him setting his sights on you."

"I don't think you need to worry about that," I say. "He's been nice to me, but he didn't hit on me at all. I doubt he'd even look at someone like me."

Juliet raises an eyebrow. "What is that supposed to mean?"

"I'm sure I'm not his type."

"Maybe not," she says. "Although, I don't know, maybe you should be. Just don't tell me you're saying that because you don't think you're pretty enough. That's ridiculous. He *wishes* he could get someone as beautiful as you."

I smile. "Thanks, Jules."

Finn comes back over, wiping a towel across the bar. "What are you girls chatting about?"

"Lucas," Juliet says.

"What about him?"

"You know, how he is with women," she says. "I was warning Becca to keep her guard up."

Finn laughs. "He's not that bad."

Juliet looks at Finn like he's crazy. "Yeah, he is."

"How so?"

"When was the last time Lucas had an actual girlfriend?" Juliet asks. "Has he ever been in a relationship? Or is it always the flavor of the week?"

"Hey," Finn says. "Lucas had a serious girlfriend when he lived in New York. They lived together. Granted, that was a few years ago, I guess."

"Well, whatever," Juliet says. "I'm not shit talking Lucas. He's great. I just don't want my sweet Becca here to be another notch on his bedpost."

I take another sip of my drink, trying not to prickle at Juliet's *my sweet Becca* comment. I don't need her to take care of me. "You don't need to worry. I can handle myself."

"Speaking of Lucas," Finn says, "I need to text him and see if we're still on for this weekend."

"Oh, that's right," Juliet says.

"What are you guys doing?" I ask.

"Lucas is taking us surfing," Juliet says, her eyes sparkling.

"Oh, wow," I say. I've never even considered going surfing—it sounds way too scary—but I'm still a little bummed they didn't invite me along.

"Who all is going?" I ask. "Just you three?"

"I'm going to drag Gabe with us," Finn says. "He'll say he has to work, but that's why we're going early. His restaurant will survive without him for a little while."

Gabe is Finn and Lucas's other good friend. He's a chef and restaurant owner. Before I moved out here, Juliet kept bugging me about coming to visit so we could have dinner at his restaurant.

"And who knows with Lucas," Juliet says. "He might bring ten other people. I'm excited. Last time we went it was so much fun, even though I was terrible at it."

Finn reaches across the bar and taps Juliet's nose. "You weren't terrible."

"No, I was objectively terrible," she says. "But it was still a good time."

At this point I can't ask to be invited—that would be too awkward. And why would I want to go surfing anyway? I'd probably end up hanging out in someone's car while they all have fun because I'd be too scared to get in the water. But I guess my disappointment shows, because Juliet puts her hand on my arm.

"Hey," she says. "You can come if you want. I didn't invite you because I figured there's no way you'd ever go surfing."

"No, it's fine," I say. "You're right. I wouldn't get in the water."

"Who's getting in the water?" Lucas says behind me.

I gasp, startled. I didn't hear him come in.

"Us, this weekend," Juliet says. "Are we still on?"

"Fuck yeah, we're on," Lucas says.

He grins at me, a crooked smile that makes him look mischievous. He's dressed in a gray t-shirt and jeans, his clothes hanging perfectly off his toned body.

*Man-whore, Becca. Not your type. You are not thinking about how ridiculously gorgeous he is.*

He sits on the stool next to me and playfully tugs on my ponytail. "Hey, neighbor."

"Hey."

Juliet gives him a weird look.

"Finn," he says. "Beer me, buddy."

Finn already has a beer for him. He hands it over and Finn lifts it up, smiling at me again.

"Cheers," he says.

I clink my glass against his beer bottle. "Cheers."

"Hey, Jules," Lucas says, holding up his beer. "So Becca, did you get the rest of your pictures hung and everything?"

"Most of them, yeah," I say. "Thanks again for your help."

"Anytime."

Juliet touches my arm, like she's trying to get my attention. "When do you start your new job?"

"Monday," I say. "I went in earlier today and met with the director again. Everything looks really great. I think I'm going to love it there."

"What do you do?" Lucas asks.

"I'm a preschool teacher."

His eyebrows lift and he starts laughing.

I set my drink down. "Are you laughing at me?"

"No," he says. "I'm not. I swear. But *of course* you're a preschool teacher."

Okay, I don't care if Lucas is cute; he's annoying me right now. I try to be nice, but it's hard to keep the edge from my voice. "What is that supposed to mean?"

"Nothing," he says with a shrug. "It just fits. I should have guessed that's what you do."

I still feel like he's making fun of me. I scowl at him and shift in my seat so he's partially behind me.

Juliet leans so she can see Lucas past me. "She's an amazing preschool teacher. She has a gift."

"I have no doubt," Lucas says. "You seem like you'd be great with kids."

He sounds sincere, and that was a nice thing to say. "Thanks. I love what I do."

"You know, that's a big deal," he says. "Too many people go through life hating their job. That's no way to live."

I turn back toward Lucas. "I agree. My parents still hint that they think I should get a better job. But I don't think I'd be happier making more money doing something else."

He tips his beer toward me. "I feel you. I have the same issue with my old man. Although I'd make *less* money doing what he wants me to do. But the whole *parental scorn* thing? I get it."

Juliet checks her phone. "I'm sorry I can't stay, but I have to drive to Seattle in the morning, so I have to get up at like five." She gets down from her stool and hugs me. "I'll text you, okay?"

"Yep. I'll see you later."

Finn comes around and gathers her up in his arms. "Night, sprinkles. I won't be too late."

I glance away while they kiss. They're so adorable. Juliet leaves and Finn goes back to the kitchen, leaving me and Lucas alone. There's no one else in the pub tonight. I feel a twinge of nervousness at being alone with him.

"So, big plans for tonight?" Lucas asks. "Are you meeting a hot date or something?"

I laugh. "Hardly. I'm happily single right now."

It's probably my imagination, but it seems like Lucas smiles a little at that.

"What about this weekend?" He nudges my arm. "Want to come surfing with us?"

"Thanks, but no." I could just tell him I'd be afraid to go surfing, but for some reason, I don't want to admit that to him. "I still have so much unpacking to do. Maybe another time."

He shrugs and takes another drink of his beer. "Fair enough."

There's a part of me that wishes he didn't drop the subject so quickly. But that's silly, because it isn't like I want to go.

I'm not sure what's wrong with me, but I'm feeling deflated. I shouldn't. It's my first week in my new apartment, in a new town, and I'm doing fine.

Maybe *fine* isn't enough. Or maybe I'm still reeling from all the changes I've made over the last several weeks. I just wish I could shake this feeling that there's something I'm missing—something more I should be doing.

I pull out some money for my drink, set it on the bar, and slide off the barstool. "I think I'm going to head home."

Lucas smiles. "Okay. I'll see you around."

"Tell Finn I said bye."

"Will do."

I head out, wondering what it's going to take to shake this feeling of being dissatisfied.

# 6

# BECCA

I go out back to get some fresh air. I have a little concrete patio with a bistro table and two chairs, so I take a seat. The sun has long since set, but the night is mild. A light breeze blows through the trees and I clutch a mug of hot tea.

It's bothering me more than it should that Juliet and Finn are going surfing with Lucas this weekend and I wasn't invited. Okay, so she did kind of invite me, but it was clearly a pity invite that she fully expected me to decline. And I said no to Lucas when he brought it up. So I shouldn't feel bad about it.

The problem is, I know Juliet's right. I would have said no. Me, in the ocean? Not a chance. That water is freezing, for one. And the waves are scary. I'm a decent swimmer, but that's in a pool—clear, chlorinated, and safe from riptides and predatory animals.

If my friend Madison were here, she'd go surfing. She's always brave. Juliet is too, in her own way. It was bravery that got her together with Finn. I wouldn't have had the guts to ask a guy to take me back to his place, like she did. And look how that turned out for her. She's supremely happy with an amazing guy.

I feel like I keep letting other people decide things for me. I always take the well-worn path. People see me as sweet and innocent, and I'm not... except I kind of am. I always play it safe. I live by the rules, color inside the lines, and do what I'm supposed to do. A lot of people explore their wild side when they're in their teens or early twenties. Me? I spent a lot of Friday and Saturday nights either at the movies with friends, or on low-key dates with nice boys my parents approved of. My parents practically hand-picked Brandon for me. Even when I lived with Madison and Juliet, I steered clear of anything that struck me as dangerous or risky.

When was the last time I did something really unexpected? I guess moving to Jetty Beach was unexpected, at least to my parents. But that's hardly a big thing. People move all the time. It's a step in the right direction, and I love the freedom I have. But it isn't enough.

I need to figure out who I am. Not who I am as a daughter, or a friend, or a girlfriend. Not who everyone else expects me to be.

I'm tired of being what they expect.

I feel like Sandy in *Grease*. The cute, naive blond girl. Maybe I need my friends to give me a slutty makeover so I can wow the bad boy and drive off into the sky in a cool car.

Okay, that last part, not so much.

I also can't help but wonder if those Internet theories about Sandy being dead the whole time are true.

But I'm getting off track.

Sandy had a wild side, didn't she? She just needed to bring it out. I'd love to think I have a wild side too. Maybe not *dress in head-to-toe black and high heels, smoking a cigarette* wild. But I wish I wasn't so scared to take risks. I wish I had the guts to go surfing. To kiss a guy I barely know, just because I want to. To do something naughty with a guy where we might get caught. To do something that scares me.

Lucas's back porch light turns on and I gasp. Crap, that startled me. The backyard is open without a barrier between my place and his. I lean back in my chair a little until I can see his sliding glass door. It looks empty inside.

Lucas appears at the door, seemingly out of nowhere, and I yelp. Crap, he scared me again. The door opens, and he steps out.

"Hey," he says with a laugh. "Sorry, did I scare you?"

God, does everything have to scare me? "Just startled me a little."

He walks over and touches the back of the other chair. "Want some company?"

"Sure."

The chair scrapes against the concrete as he pulls it away from the table. He sits down. "So, how do you like living at the beach so far?"

"It's good," I say. "My apartment is nice, and I think my job is going to be great. This was a good move for me."

He nods. "Awesome. It's nice having someone normal live next door. The guy before you was a real weirdo."

"Was he?"

"Yeah," Lucas says. "He liked to cook, but he burnt everything, so the smoke alarms went off at least a few times a week. And he was a really loud talker. I heard all his phone conversations. That was awkward."

"Well, I guess now you have me."

He grins and it sends a tingle down my spine. "That I do, darling. And I've already had the pleasure of getting you to say a naughty word."

I laugh. "You're hoping I'll say it again right now, aren't you?"

"Kinda."

I nibble on my bottom lip for a second and glance away. "Fuck."

Lucas laughs. "I don't know why that's so much fun, but it really is."

"I'm glad to be your amusement tonight."

"Why are you so squeamish about swearing, anyway?" he asks. "Strict parents?"

"Yeah, I suppose they were," I say. "They never swore and I wasn't allowed to see R-rated movies until... well, I didn't see one until after I moved out and went to college, if that tells you anything. It's just not in my nature. They raised me to be a lady."

"Yeah, but you can be a lady and still say fuck and stuff," he says. "In this day and age, there's no reason to be stuffy."

"I'm not stuffy!"

"No, I didn't mean you are," he says. "And there's a time and a place for more rigid manners. But hey, we're just hanging out on a nice evening. What's a little fuck between friends?"

I cross my legs to suppress the rush of arousal at his comment. I'm glad it's dark out here, because I'm positive I'm blushing like crazy. He's smiling like he's trying to get a rise out of me.

But thinking about swearing—and Lucas—is giving me an idea.

I need someone to do the slutty makeover, except not with big hair and leather. And not *actually* slutty. Just... someone who can help me be a little more daring. Take a few risks. Lucas got me to say the f-word for the first time in my life. Maybe he can help me do a few more things to loosen up a little.

Because the problem is, I have no idea where to start.

"Have you seen *Grease*?" I ask, before I lose my nerve.

Lucas sings, "Summer lovin', had me a blast."

He *sings*.

And he's really good.

"Wow," I say. "Impressive."

He laughs. "Thanks. It's one of my karaoke favorites. But yeah, I've seen it. Why?"

"Will you promise not to a laugh at me?"

"At this point, I don't think I can promise anything of the sort."

"Come on, give me a break," I say. "I might need your help with something. But this is kind of embarrassing."

He leans forward in his chair. "Now I'm intrigued. Okay, I won't laugh."

I take a deep breath. "This might come as a surprise to you, but I'm basically Sandy."

He tilts his head and looks at me. "Holy shit, you are."

I roll my eyes. "Sort of. I'm not exactly like Sandy, and I haven't had a summer fling with a bad boy who's actually really sweet or whatever. But I do have the tendency to play it safe."

"I have no idea where you're going with this, but I'm fascinated right now," he says.

"Are you making fun of me?"

"No," he says with a laugh. "Go on."

"Well, you were right about swearing," I say. "I'd never actually uttered that word before."

"Fuck?"

"Yes, that one."

"You should say it again, right now," he says.

"Oh my god, focus," I say. "This isn't about swearing. I'm living totally on my own for the first time, and that's great. But I'm still missing something. I think I miss out on a lot of things because I'm too timid to take chances."

"I can see that," he says.

"I want to, I don't know, loosen up," I say. "Take a few risks. Nothing huge. I don't want to do anything really foolish or get hurt. But maybe bring out my naughty side. Just a tiny bit."

Lucas clears his throat and shifts in his seat. "So, why are you telling me?"

"The problem is, I don't know where to start," I say. "Just saying a bad word isn't all that risky. But I can't think of what else I'd do. So, I was wondering if you had any ideas."

"Ideas to bring out your naughty side?"

"Yeah, sort of. I want to be more like Sandy at the end of *Grease*, rather than the beginning."

"Can we dress you in black leather and heels?" he asks.

I laugh. "No, clothes aren't the point."

Lucas puts a hand to his chin and looks out over the dark yard for a long moment. "Yeah, I have a few ideas."

A twinge of nervousness zings through me. I wonder if I'm going to regret this. I barely know Lucas. Maybe I should have asked Juliet. But I have a feeling Juliet's version of helping me be naughty wouldn't be enough.

"Okay, cool," I say.

"How do you feel about tequila?" he asks.

I laugh. "Tequila is great, especially in margarita form. I've been drunk lots of times, if that's what you're hinting at. I'm not *that* innocent."

"Damn, I was kind of hoping I'd be able to get you drunk for the first time," he says. "That would be fun. Oh well, maybe we'll get drunk anyway."

I shrug. "Maybe."

"You know what? You did the right thing in coming to me. This is going to be fun."

I bite my lower lip and my hands feel shaky. "Yeah?"

"Absolutely," he says. "But tell me first, what are your rules? Do you have any hard limits?"

"Well, yeah," I say. "I don't want to break the law or do anything that could get me into trouble."

"Hmm," he says. "Agreed about law-breaking. Mostly. But we might have to push the boundaries of getting in trouble, just a little."

"But—"

"Hey," he says, putting his finger up. "Naughty side, right? Some rules can be bent. You'll see."

"Fine, but nothing that's going to mess up my life in any significant way," I say.

"No, of course not," he says. "What you need is to have a few adventures. New experiences. You need to face your fears."

"Yes, that's exactly it. But like I said, I don't know where to start."

He tilts his head and grins at me. "This is going to be amazing. I think I'm really going to enjoy dirtying you up a little."

Oh my god. He did *not* just say that, and my panties did *not* just get wet.

Okay, yes they did.

"Just be gentle with me," I say. "I'm a fraidy-cat."

He smiles again and my insides turn to mush. "Darling, you have nothing to worry about. I'm going to take excellent care of you."

# 7

# LUCAS

I jot down a few notes as I sip my afternoon coffee. Work was stressful as hell, but I came out ahead at the end of the day. My profits and losses can swing pretty wildly from one hour to the next. I'm used to that. Market conditions today, however, tested my aversion to risk. Thankfully, I trusted my instincts, and they didn't steer me wrong. I went from losing about five grand, to being ahead by two, so that's a big win.

Becca's front door closes with a bang. She's right, the walls are thin. I guess she's home from work. I shake my head thinking about her. The sweet preschool teacher. I can picture her sitting in a chair in front of a bunch of four-year-olds, reading a story.

It seems it's my task to help the good girl find her bad side.

I'm actually stoked that she asked me. Surprised, but glad. She wants me to help bring out the bad girl? I can definitely do that.

The question is, where do I begin?

At first, I figured this would be easy. Take her out, get her drunk, maybe convince her to do something crazy like skinny dipping in the lake next to the golf course. But I have to be careful with this. There were about five times during our conversation where not only did my dick stand up and pay attention, my thoughts immediately went somewhere they shouldn't. Bad girl? Oh, baby, I'll show you how to be bad.

But I know she didn't mean it that way, and sleeping with her is not a good idea. She's way too sweet of a girl to want what I have to offer. Granted, she'd love every second of it, but I'm sure she'd want the relationship trappings to go along with it. And I'm definitely not going there.

I need to think of ways to get her out of her comfort zone that don't involve me getting her naked. Not *quite* as much fun, but I'm looking forward to it anyway.

I do have an idea for where to begin. It's not so much *bad girl* as it is making her do something she might not otherwise do. Face her fears. I send Finn a quick text and get up to grab a bite to eat and change before I head out to put my plan into action.

∾

I'M GREETED by a buzz of conversation as I push open the door to Finn's pub. The place is packed, which is perfect. For what I have planned, we need an audience.

Becca is sitting with Juliet at a small table off to the side. I grin at both of them, but head to the bar first. I need to talk to Finn.

Finn comes out from the kitchen. "Hey, man."

"Hey. Are we good for tonight? I know it's not a Saturday, but I have a reason."

"Yeah, it's fine with me," he says. "Are you going to tell me what you're up to, or am I just playing along?"

"I'm just doing something with Becca."

Juliet appears next to me, out of nowhere. "What about Becca?"

"Where did you come from?" I glance around, but I don't see Becca.

"I came from over there," Juliet says. "But why are you talking about Becca?"

I smile at her. I see what she's doing—that girl thing where they circle the wagons when they perceive a threat to one of their own. "Why shouldn't I be talking about Becca?"

She raises an eyebrow. "You be good, Lucas Murphy."

I put my hands up. "What? Why would you think I'd be anything else?"

"Because I know you," she says.

"You don't have anything to worry about."

"Becca just had her heart ripped to shreds. Don't you dare mess with her. Or…"

I laugh and Juliet glares at me. "Or what?"

"I don't know, but it'll be something bad."

I just wink at her. "Okay. I'm going to get out the karaoke machine."

Jesse, one of the pub employees, helps me get things set up. I notice Becca come out of the restroom, and she stares at me for a long moment before going back to her table with Juliet. I chuckle to myself.

I go back to the bar while Jesse gets the first singer started on a song. I order two shots of vanilla vodka with a splash of cherry to make them go down easy; I figure that will give Becca one less reason to object than if I brought her a shot of whiskey or something. I carry them over to Juliet and Becca's table and take a seat.

"Hi, ladies." I slide one of the shots over to Becca.

"What's this for?" she asks.

"Liquid courage."

"Lucas, what are you doing?" Juliet asks.

I ignore her and keep looking at Becca. I lift my shot. "Come on. Down it."

"I want to know why," she says.

I hold her gaze and smile. "Trust me."

She narrows her eyes at me, but lifts her shot glass and drinks. I swallow mine.

The first guy finishes his song and the other customers give him a round of applause. He didn't sound too bad. The next singer takes the microphone and the music starts up again.

I turn to Becca and hold out my hand. "You ready?"

She eyes me with suspicion. "Ready for what?"

"Our turn."

"Oh, no," she says. "I'm not singing."

"Do you want another shot first?" I ask.

"No."

"New experiences, Becca." I stand and hold out my hand again. "I know it's scary, but you need to face some fears."

"I can't get up in front of everyone," she says. "And I'm not a good singer."

"That's okay, we'll do it together. Come on, it's just karaoke. No one expects you to be good."

Her brow furrows and she chews on her lower lip.

"It's okay, Becca," Juliet says. "You really don't have to."

Becca straightens and slips her hand in mine. "Fine. I'll do it."

"Awesome."

I lead Becca across the pub, tossing a wink over my

shoulder at Juliet as we walk away. She watches us go, her mouth hanging open.

We get to what passes for a stage—it's really just an area where there's room for a few people to stand with a wall at their back. The last singer hands me his microphone, and Jesse gives Becca the second one.

She pops up on her tiptoes and speaks into my ear. "What are we singing?"

"*I Love Rock and Roll*," I say. "Everyone loves Joan Jett. Trust me. Act a little silly and have fun with it, and half the place will start singing along."

Her brow furrows, and she clutches the microphone with both hands, but she nods. I give Jesse a wave to get the song started.

The music begins and at first, it's mostly me singing. Becca holds the mic too far from her mouth for it to pick up her voice, and she watches the screen for the lyrics. A few people start clapping along. Just before the chorus hits, I nudge her and smile.

She brings the mic closer and sings along, half laughing. By the second round of the chorus, most of the other customers are yelling the words and fist pumping in the air along with Becca. Finn whoops from behind the bar, and I catch a glimpse of Juliet smiling and clapping to the beat of the music.

The song ends, and everyone cheers. I hold up Becca's arm, like she just won first place. Her cheeks are pink, her eyes sparkling—her smile lights up her whole face. We clasp hands and give a dramatic bow.

I take the mic and give them both back to Jesse, then grab Becca in a big hug. People reach out and give her high fives while we walk back to her table on the other side of the pub.

"I can't believe I just did that," she says with a laugh.

I nudge her with my elbow. "See? I knew you could do it. And was it fun?"

"Yeah, it was really fun."

"Want to do another song?" I ask.

She raises her eyebrows and chews on her lower lip again. I'm mostly kidding—my plan was to get her up there once—but the spunky little thing is thinking about it.

"Okay, let's do it," she says. "But maybe I should have another drink first."

"Darling, I have you covered."

Four songs—and I'm not sure how many drinks—later, neither of us are in any shape to drive, so Juliet takes us home. Juliet gives me the side-eye when she says goodnight, and I half expect her to get out and take Becca up to her door.

Becca and I walk up to the path that separates our two front doors.

"Hey, you." I step closer, and I'm almost drunk enough that I grab her and kiss her. But I stop myself before I make that mistake. Although I'm having trouble remembering why it would be a mistake. "You were awesome tonight."

"Thanks," she says with a giggle. "I hope I don't regret anything tomorrow."

I wave my hand, like it's no big thing. "Nah. You won't. We sang a few songs, and we avoided anything by the *Spice Girls*. Nothing to regret."

She laughs and fiddles with her keys. Damn it, she's giving me all the right signals. I could absolutely kiss her right now, and she'd be totally into it. I could take her into my place, and fuck her brains out. Better yet, I could take her into *her* apartment, and fuck her brains out on *her* bed.

Oh my god, I bet her sheets are pink. It's almost too tempting to resist.

But she hiccups and covers her mouth with her hand, reminding me that she's pretty tossed. Plus, she's on my off-limits list for a reason. We have to be neighbors. She might not regret singing karaoke in front of a bunch of people, but she'd probably regret sleeping with me. We had an awesome night together, and I don't want to ruin it.

"We should both crash," I say. "Will you make it inside okay?"

Fine, I'm leaving an opening in case she invites me in.

She takes a step back. "Oh, yeah. I'm good."

"All right." I step back, putting a little more distance between us before I lose my mind and pounce on her. "I'll see you later."

"Good night, Lucas," she says. "And thanks."

I point at her. "Hey, thank *you*. Tonight was fun."

She smiles and takes the few steps to her door. I wait until she unlocks it and goes inside.

Her door shuts and I blow out a long breath. My head is swimming, like I used up the last of my faculties saying goodnight. I go inside, stumble upstairs, and fall into bed still dressed—kind of disappointed I'm alone.

## 8

## BECCA

My stomach is a little queasy when I get home from my run. It's hotter than usual—the sky is clear and there's no breeze coming off the ocean. My shirt sticks to my skin and a bead of sweat tickles my neck. I need water—and a shower.

I glance at Lucas's door. I haven't seen him since Friday night when he convinced me to sing Karaoke with him at the pub. Far from regretting it the next day, I woke up Saturday morning with a sense of satisfaction. I've always been scared to get up in front of people—forget *singing* in front of people. I've never liked being the center of attention. But with Lucas, it was fun. I felt so... free. Free to be silly, and have a good time. The drinks helped, I'm sure, but it was more than getting tipsy. I've been drunk with friends before, and wouldn't have dreamed of getting up in front of everyone with a microphone.

It was scary, but I'm glad I did it. I still don't feel like I've conquered my fraidy-cat side, but I'm one step closer.

My phone vibrates in my shorts pocket, so I pull it out and check. It's a text from my dad. *Another* one. He texted me when I first went out for my run and I made the mistake of telling him what I was doing. About five minutes later, I got a freaking dissertation—via at least six messages because it went on so long—explaining why I should join a gym or find a running partner (preferably female) instead of going out for a run on my own.

I can almost hear the urgency in his latest text. *Are you home yet, princess? Check in when you're back.*

A part of me is tempted not to text him. I love my dad, but even from three hours away, he's smothering me. I understand that I'm his little girl, and he worries. But I wish he'd trust me enough to let me live my life. I don't need to check in with my parents every time I go running.

Still, it would be mean not to reply. *Yes, Dad, I'm back. No one kidnapped me on my way home.*

He won't think that's funny, but I can't help myself.

I need to figure out how to set some better boundaries with my parents. Although living this far away does help. My dad might text me a lot, but he can't show up unexpectedly "just to check on me." I love having space to myself.

I head inside and get some water, then go upstairs to take a shower.

I strip off my sweaty running clothes in my bedroom and wrap a fluffy towel around myself. The towels were a housewarming gift from Juliet, and they're awesome—thick and pure white, like you'd get at a spa. I go into the bathroom, turn on the shower, and wait for the water to get hot.

After a minute, steam billows from the shower stall. I open the door and just as I'm about to take off my towel, I spot it on the ceiling.

A huge, black, disgusting spider.

I shriek before I can stop myself and clap a hand over my

mouth. Oh my god. I hate spiders. I don't just hate them. I'm terrified of them. Lots of people don't like spiders. Me? As far as I'm concerned, they're the most hideous creatures in existence and every last one of them is out to kill me. I can barely even look at a spider on TV, let alone face one down in the shower.

I slam the shower door shut. The water is still running, but there's nothing I can do about that now. There's a fricking spider in there. It's not some small, normal spider, either. It's legitimately enormous.

I adjust the towel around myself and take a deep breath. If I'm going to take care of myself, that means I need to be able to get rid of a spider. I repeat to myself what other people always say: *They're more scared of you than you are of them.*

Right about now, I really doubt that.

It was on the ceiling, so I run downstairs and get a broom. Yes, this is good. I can reach it without getting close. I can do this.

I tip-toe my way into the bathroom, like it's lying in wait, ready to pounce on me. After taking a deep breath, I open the shower door. I bite my lip to keep from shrieking again. It's still there.

With my hands clutching the broom handle, I inch closer.

"Okay, spider, I live here, which means you can't. I'm really sorry about this, but there just isn't room for both of us in this apartment."

I get closer and the horrible thing moves. I squeal and jump backward, my heart beating furiously.

*Come on, Becca. Don't let the spider win.*

I tighten my grip on the broom and get closer. The spider's spindly legs twitch, but I force myself to keep moving toward it. With the bottom of the broom pointing up, I get ready to thrust it at the ceiling.

I slam the broom against the ceiling, but the evil thing scurries into a corner. My heart hammers, and I hesitate for few seconds.

Just as I'm about to try again, the spider runs. Toward me.

I scream, drop the broom, and fly down the stairs and out my front door.

I bang on Lucas's door and realize too late that I'm only wearing a towel. I hold it up at my chest, panicking. Maybe I should run back inside. But I already knocked. His door starts to open.

*Oh, no.*

Lucas's eyes widen when he sees me. He opens his mouth to say something, but I start talking, the words spilling out fast.

"There's a huge spider in my shower, and I tried to get it myself, but I swear it was going to attack me, so I ran."

Lucas laughs. *Of course* he laughs at me. He leans against the door, clutching his stomach, practically doubling over.

"Stop it," I say. "It's not funny."

"I'm sorry." He straightens and puts up a hand. "Don't be mad. You're just... are you naked under there?"

My face heats up and I hold the towel tighter. "You know what? Never mind. I just won't use my bathroom until it goes away." I turn and march toward my door.

"No, Becca, wait. I'm sorry. I'll help." He catches up and I let him follow me into my apartment. "All right, let's just see what we've got."

I move aside so he can go upstairs first. I don't want to go back into the bathroom at all, but I need to make sure he really kills it. The last thing I need is for him to think it would be funny to tell me it's gone, but leave it somewhere for me to find. I shudder, a cold shiver running down my back.

"It was in your shower?" Lucas asks when we get to the bathroom. "The water's running. Maybe you already drowned it."

"No, it's on the ceiling."

I hesitate in the doorway while he picks up the broom. He opens the shower door, then slams it shut again.

"Holy shit," he says.

"What?"

He takes a step back. "That's a huge fucking spider."

"I told you."

"Okay, I have to be honest with you," he says. "I hate spiders. I thought it was going to be one of those little ones. That thing is a fucking beast."

"I know! Kill it!"

He adjusts his grip on the broom and shoots me a glare. I hold the towel and chew on my thumbnail while he creeps toward the shower. He glances over his shoulder at me again, his jaw set, before he throws open the shower door.

Lucas stabs at the ceiling with the broom. "Fuck!"

I shriek and back up into the hall. "What happened?"

"The little fucker moved. He's a quick son of a bitch."

He stabs a few more times and I hold my hand over my mouth so I don't scream again.

"Ha! Got you, little bastard." He pokes the bottom of the broom on the floor a couple times, like he's making sure the vile creature is dead.

I step back into the doorway. "Did you get it?"

"Yep." He nods toward the floor in front of the sink. "Smashed the shit out of it."

I take a deep breath. "Thank you."

"You're wel—" He looks at me and his eyes widen again.

My towel is starting to fall open. "Oh, crap." I grab it with both hands, and I'm sure I'm blushing from head to toe.

Lucas chuckles and leans the broom against the counter. "Okay, darling. I think your spider infestation is handled. I'll leave you to your shower. Although I'm not sure if there's much hot water left."

He's probably right. Figures. I move aside while he comes out of the bathroom and walks past me.

He pauses at the top of the stairs and gives me a sly grin. "If you want to come next door and shower, I can help with that too."

"Bye, Lucas."

He laughs and heads downstairs. "Bye, Becca."

I lean against the door frame and breathe out a long breath. Stupid spider. Stupid Lucas. Although I'm glad he killed it for me. He didn't have to laugh at me quite so much, but it was kind of satisfying to see him creeped out by it too.

I turn off the water. I'll have to wait to take a shower. There's no way I'm going next door to shower at Lucas's place. If I did, he might—

I stop that train of thought right in its tracks. I'm not even going to *think* it. I'm not going over there right now. I'm not the least bit tempted.

Nope. Not at all.

9

# LUCAS

The pizza smells awesome. I pay the delivery guy and bring them inside. I ordered two, since I'm not sure what Becca likes. I could have asked her ahead of time, but it's more fun to spring things on her.

I send her a text. *Wanna come over? I have pizza and a movie.*

I've been hanging out with Becca a lot lately. It's easy with her right next door. We sit around and watch random shit on Netflix, or run out to the store together. It turns out she's an amazing cook, and she invites me over for dinner all the time. My version of cooking is usually heating up something from a can, so all these home cooked meals are fantastic.

Tonight, I figured I could handle dinner. Plus, I have something else up my sleeve.

She texts me back. *Give me five minutes, k?*

I answer back—*See you in a few*—and unlock the back door for her.

Since our karaoke night, I've come up with a few more ways to help Becca come out of her shell. Mostly I've been making her face her fears. There was a spider in my apartment—thankfully a much smaller one—and I convinced her to squish it with a paper towel. Last weekend, I took her out to a hiking spot that leads to a suspension bridge. She was nervous to walk out over the ravine, and it took a few minutes of coaxing. But I held her hand and led the way, and I have to give her credit—she kept her eyes open. By the time we reached the other side and had to turn around and go back, she walked ahead of me and even stopped in the middle to look down.

She's not nearly as afraid as she thinks she is. She just needs someone to reassure her that she can do things she's never tried before.

Someone like me, I guess.

The back door opens and Becca comes in. She's wearing a pair of light gray shorts and a white t-shirt. I try to keep my eyes off her toned legs.

That sounds easier than it is.

"Hey." She closes the door behind her. "I'm glad you texted. I didn't feel like cooking tonight."

"Awesome." I get some paper plates out of a cupboard. "Is everything okay?"

"Yeah, I'm just tired," she says. "Work took a lot out of me."

"Little stinkers giving you trouble?"

She laughs. "One little stinker. She's a sweetheart, but I think she's having some turmoil at home, so she's acting up in class. She kept at it, so eventually I got out the play dough to keep the rest of the kids busy and sat with her in the reading chair. I think the poor little thing just needed a hug."

Becca's stories about work have a strange tendency to tug

at my heartstrings a little. "You must be amazing with those kids."

She smiles. "Thanks."

I gesture to the pizza. "I ordered from Roma's, which means it's greasy as hell, but delicious. There's a pepperoni and sausage, and a supreme that looks like it has a little of everything."

She comes around the counter into the kitchen and eyes both pizzas. "I'll take one of each."

"That's my girl." I nudge her with my elbow. I love that she actually eats. I've been with too many girls who don't seem to.

Of course, I'm not *with* Becca. But still.

We load up our plates and I grab a roll of paper towels—Roma's pizza is messy. We settle in on the couch. Becca tucks her legs up and sets her plate on her thighs.

"How about you?" she asks. "Make tons of money today?"

"I did all right. I made up for my loss yesterday, so that's a good way to end the week."

"Your job would stress me out," she says. "I don't know how you do it."

I shrug. "I like it. It's like solving a puzzle every day. I have to predict what's going to happen and bet on the conclusions I draw."

"I'll take my snotty-nosed four-year-olds," she says.

She takes a bite of her pizza and laughs as grease drips down her chin. I grab a paper towel and wipe it off for her. Her eyes meet mine and I realize how close we're sitting. Our legs are almost touching. It makes my heart beat faster and my dick stand up and pay attention.

There's no way I can deny the pings of sexual tension

that spark between us whenever we're together. She feels it too—I can see it in her eyes.

It's moments like this I wish she wasn't my neighbor.

Although, that's not entirely true. I love it when she shows up at my back door and waves at me through the glass. I wouldn't have that if she didn't live next door. Or when I come up with something random to do that might scare her, and I get to be the one to coax her into it. She's fun to hang out with. I don't know that I've ever had this kind of relationship with a woman before, but I like it. It's so easy with Becca. We can spend time together, do all kinds of cool shit, and there's no drama.

That's enough to get me to back off. I like Becca—I like her as more than a hot piece of ass. Sure, she's beautiful. She has a fantastic body, and I jerk off to Becca fantasies pretty much every night. But she's more than that. She's fun and sweet and I like being around her. I wouldn't want to jeopardize that.

She shifts so that there are a few more inches between us. "So, movie night?"

"Yes." I set my plate down on the coffee table. "I have a treat for you."

"Uh-oh," she says.

"What do you mean, uh-oh?"

"You're up to something," she says. "I can tell."

"I am not up to something," I say. She narrows her eyes at me. "Okay, that's a lie. We're going to watch a horror movie."

She freezes in place and her eyes widen. The color drains from her face. "What movie?"

"Well, we have options," I say. "But I'm thinking *Poltergeist*. Unless you've already seen it."

She shakes her head.

"Awesome. It's a classic." I grab the remote and turn on the TV.

"Lucas, I don't think I want to watch a horror movie," she says. Her voice is quiet.

"Have you ever seen one before?"

Her eyes dart to the TV, then back to me. "Not really. But I don't think this is necessary."

"It's good to face your fears," I say. "How did you feel on that bridge? Or in front of everyone when we were singing?"

She takes a deep breath. "Scared at first."

I hold up a finger. "At first. What about after?"

"I was… okay, maybe a little exhilarated."

"Maybe a little?" I ask. "I saw your face, darling. On that bridge you lit up like the sun. You conquered that shit, and you were proud of yourself."

Her mouth turns up in a little smile. "Okay, that's true. I *was* proud of myself."

"See? And the more times you do things like that—even small things like watching a scary movie—the more you'll feel brave other times. You'll remember how it felt to conquer that bridge, or the mic, or a movie, and the next thing you want to try won't seem so scary anymore."

She nibbles on her lower lip. "All right, I'll watch on one condition."

"What's that?"

"No making fun of me if I scream."

I laugh. "That's fair. I won't tease you at all."

I turn on the movie and we go back to our dinner. The beginning of the movie is mellow, and to be honest, it's pretty dated. I have a feeling once things get going, it won't scare her very much. We finish our pizza and I get us a couple beers.

Introducing her to beer is another of my triumphs.

Becca discovered, to her surprise, that as long as it's not too dark or heavy, she likes it. And a girl who can enjoy a good beer is a special kind of sexy.

I watch her take a sip, tilting the bottle to her lips. Those full, pink lips.

Maybe teaching her to like beer wasn't the best move.

I shift so I can adjust my dick, hopefully without her noticing. But her eyes are glued to the screen.

The movie gets creepier, and Becca pulls a pillow into her lap. I watch her from the corner of my eye. She's curled up with her toes tucked into the seam between the cushions, her arms clutching the pillow tight to her chest. She chews on her lip and her eyes widen. I get the feeling she wants to cover her eyes a few times, but her gaze flicks to me, and she doesn't.

We get to the part where the tree comes after the kid, and Becca abandons the pillow and grabs my arm. She buries her face against me and peeks out at the screen. I try really hard not to laugh.

She spends the rest of the movie snuggled against me and digging her fingers into my arm. I turn my face slightly and breathe in her scent. She always smells so good—lightly floral and clean. Believe it or not, watching a scary movie wasn't a ploy to get her to touch me like this. In fact, it's kind of killing me. She feels so good against me and it's hard not to put my arms around her.

When the movie ends, she lets go of my arm and scoots away, like she just realized what she was doing. I don't want to make her uncomfortable, so I play it off like we didn't just spend the last half hour practically cuddling.

"So, what did you think?"

"I don't know, that was really scary," she says.

"But you watched the whole thing," I say. "You rocked it, darling."

"I think I bruised your arm."

I hold out my arm and turn it over. "I'll live."

"Okay, yes, I watched it, but I think I can safely say I don't like scary movies," she says. "That was too stressful."

Damn it, now I feel bad. "I'm sorry. I didn't think this one would bother you that much."

"No, don't be sorry." She touches her hand to her chest. "I just wish my heart would quit beating so fast."

"How about this," I say. "It's not that late, and tomorrow's Saturday. Let's watch another, and you pick. Anything you want."

Her eyes light up. "Really? Anything?"

"Anything at all."

She smiles. "Okay, I'll be right back."

She heads out the back door and returns a few minutes later with a bag of kettle corn in one hand and a movie in the other. She puts the bag down on the coffee table and clutches the movie to her chest.

"This is an important moment," she says. "This is my absolute favorite movie ever, and if you tell me you don't like it, I don't know if we can still be friends."

I hear the joke in her voice, but I've already resolved to tell her I love the movie, even if I hate it.

She turns it around. *The Princess Bride.*

"As you wish," I say.

She blinks with a look of surprise and I realize I sort of just said *I love you* without meaning to.

I clear my throat, anxious to brush that off. "That's a great movie. I can't remember the last time I saw it, though."

"Perfect," she says. "This is always what I watch when I'm stressed or upset."

"Let's do it."

We watch Becca's movie, munching on kettle corn. She clearly knows the entire thing by heart. I see her lips move with the lines throughout most of it. The movie is genuinely good, but it's even more fun seeing her enjoy it.

So, maybe no more scary movies. But I still have some other ideas. As much as I like casually hanging out with Becca, I like pushing her too. My next idea might prove to be the thing that pushes her too hard. But I need to draw out her naughty side, and I think I have a way to do it.

## 10

## BECCA

I'm putting away my dishes when a few taps at my back door startle me. Lucas is standing outside holding a couple of plastic grocery bags. He grins at me as I come to let him in.

"Hey." He sets the bags on the coffee table and starts pulling things out. There's a bag of Doritos, a big package of Oreo cookies, a bag of gummy bears, a bottle of blue Gatorade, and a half gallon of milk.

"What is all this?" I ask.

"We're going to need this later," he says.

I glance at the pile of junk food on the coffee table. "For what?"

He looks at me and a big grin steals over his face. I'm starting to become familiar with that look, and it sends a flurry of butterflies swirling through my stomach. He has something planned. I don't know if I should be excited, or scared.

Probably both.

Lucas reaches into his jacket and pulls out a small

plastic bag. It has what looks a bit like two whitish crayons, but they're blank, and a little too lumpy.

Uh-oh. I know what those are.

He holds up the bag, waving it in front of me. "I'm going to get you high."

I know the burst of terror I feel is plain on my face, but I can't help it. "You're going to *what*?"

"Have you ever smoked weed before?" he asks.

"No."

"I didn't think so," he says.

"But..." I take a step backward "I can't smoke pot."

"Why not?"

I put my hands on my hips. "Because... I just can't."

He grins at me again. "Of course you can. It's even legal here. I bought these at a store."

I open my mouth to argue, but I'm not sure what else to say. I've never smoked pot. I've been drunk plenty of times; I'm not a total ingénue. But pot wasn't legal until pretty recently, and it was always on my *no way* list. Good girls don't get high.

"Oh my god, Lucas, I can't believe I'm thinking about agreeing to this."

"Of course you're agreeing to this," he says. "It's going to be fun as shit."

I look at the food again. "Are we really going to eat all that?"

"Maybe," he says. "We shouldn't drive if we're high, so I figured I'd be prepared with some supplies."

"I guess this means you've done this before?" I ask.

"Yep."

I look him up and down. "How do you stay in such good shape if you eat like this?"

He laughs. "I've done it before, but I can't remember the last time I got high. Probably college. But I figure you, my little darling, have never been baked, and we need to change that."

I bite my lip and sink down onto the edge of the couch. Should I do this? I'm the one who wanted Lucas to help me find my naughty side. What's naughtier than getting high?

Well, several things, but I'm not doing any of those with Lucas, so I can stop thinking about that right now.

I take a deep breath and sit on the couch. "Okay."

"Awesome." He sits down next to me and grabs the bag. "You should probably give me your phone for the night."

"Why?"

"Do you want to have the ability to text your friends and post who knows what on Facebook while we're baked out of our gourds? I sprang for some good shit, here."

"I don't think I want to do this anymore," I say, but I hand him my phone.

He laughs and nudges me with his elbow. Actually, it's more than a nudge. He rubs his arm against mine and the feel of his skin brushing against me makes my heart beat faster.

"You're going to be fine." He turns and meets my eyes, and when he speaks again, his voice is softer. "I won't let anything bad happen to you. Trust me."

I hate it when he looks at me like that. It sends all these little swirls of nervousness through my whole body. His eyes hold onto mine, and I can't look away—which means I notice all the things about him that make my heart flutter. His chiseled jaw. His piercing eyes. His broad chest.

"Pot doesn't make you..." I don't know how to ask this, or even if I should. "You know."

"No, I don't know. Make you what?"

I look away. I can't look him in the eyes and say this. "Horny?"

Lucas laughs. We laugh a lot together, but this time, I'm not laughing with him.

"I'm sorry, I just didn't expect you to say that." He shrugs. "Probably not. But don't worry, I'm not going to take advantage of you or anything. Even when we're high."

Of course he's not, because Lucas doesn't look at me that way. He's probably starting to think of me as a little sister. That thought is oddly depressing. Is that how he sees me? Like someone completely outside the realm of sexual attraction?

But why do I care? I'm not attracted to him. Nope. Not at all.

I need to get this over with.

"Okay, let's do this before I lose my nerve," I say. "Although, are we going to smoke it inside?"

"Well, I do know your landlord pretty well, and I don't think he's going to get mad," he says with a grin. "But if you're worried about the smell, we can do it out back and then come in."

I'm so nervous, my hands are trembling, but I follow Lucas out the back door to the small concrete patio. We sit on either side of my bistro table, and Lucas pulls out a lighter.

"Ready?" he asks.

"No."

He just laughs and lights the end of the joint. He takes a long drag and pulls the end out of his mouth, hesitating for several seconds before exhaling. The pungent sweet smell wafts over to me and I resist the urge to cough and wave my hand in front of my face.

"I have no idea how to do this. I've never even smoked a cigarette." My eyes widen. "Oh, no. You aren't going to make me do that too, are you?"

Lucas shakes his head. "Nah, there's nothing exciting about cigarettes. Plus, they stink."

*And this doesn't?* Although the smell isn't completely unpleasant. It's sort of earthy with a hint of something sweet, almost like berries.

"All right, darling," he says, holding the joint out to me across the table. "Your turn."

I take it from him and pinch it between my thumb and index finger.

"Just put the tip in your mouth and suck in a little," Lucas says.

Please tell me it's normal that the first thing I think of is his cock in my mouth. That's what anyone would think upon hearing the phrase *put the tip in your mouth and suck*, right?

No? Just me?

I put the joint between my lips and suck some air through it. The smoke slides through my mouth and into my lungs. At first I'm afraid I'll cough and choke, but it's smoother than I thought it would be. I try to mimic Lucas and hold my breath for a few seconds before exhaling, but I don't last very long. I blow out the smoke, marveling at the look of it as it clouds in front of my face.

Holy shit. I just did that.

I also said *shit* in my head, like it's part of my normal vocabulary.

I pass the joint back to Lucas and he takes a longer drag, then blows it out. "See, this isn't so scary."

He's right, it isn't scary. In fact, I don't feel a thing. I look around the dark yard, expecting to be hit with a sudden sense of... something. Euphoria? Giggles? Hunger? But I feel totally normal.

"Here, have a little more," he says.

I take another hit and blow out the smoke. It's easier this time. I sit back in my chair and try to analyze whether I'm feeling high or not. I still can't tell.

"Should I feel something yet?" I ask.

"Give it a minute." He takes another drag.

We pass the joint back and forth a couple more times. I watch Lucas lick his lips before he puts it between them. They press together as he breathes in. His mouth is fascinating. It's almost like he's moving in slow motion. He puts the joint down and blows out the smoke, then turns and gives me a lazy smile.

"What do you think?"

"I don't feel anything," I say. "But you know what's weird? I don't smell it anymore. At first, I could totally smell the smoke, but it's like now I can't. Why is that? It has such a strong smell, but somehow it's just gone."

He drags his teeth over his lower lip and touches my hand. "That's because you're high."

"But I'm really not. I feel so normal. Although I'm wondering why you didn't buy a building closer to the beach. We can't even hear the waves from here. What is it, about a mile walk? Have you ever walked to the beach from here? Does the road go straight there, or do you have to take a lot of turns? Because that would make it longer."

Lucas laughs and trails his finger over the back of my hand. "You're so fucking high. It's making you all talky."

I snatch my hand away. "I have no idea what you're talking about. I'm not talky. I'm normal. This is me, all the time. I'm always like this. I don't feel—"

I stop mid-sentence, because not only do I realize he's right—it *is* making me talky—I don't feel normal. Not at all.

It's as if all my muscles are uncoiling, releasing little knots of tension I didn't even know were there. My back loosens, and my limbs feel light. The beginning of a headache I had earlier is completely gone and a sense of calmness steals over me. My mind is clear, relaxed, and yet somehow buzzing with thought. I open my mouth, but stop myself from talking again. I'm still aware enough to know that if I start, I'll launch into another barrage of sentences that may or may not make any sense.

I don't actually hallucinate—I'm not really seeing things that aren't there—but it seems as if there are little flares of light in the air, just at the edges of my vision. It's intriguing, and I blink a few times, trying to bring them into focus.

Lucas is still smiling at me.

"What?" I ask. The urge to keep talking seems to be fading, because I don't say anything else.

He laughs and rests his head against the back of the chair. His eyes are sleepy and he taps his fingers absently on the table. "Nothing. How do you feel?"

"Really good." My voice sounds odd and far away. "I'm so relaxed. I feel like… like I don't care about anything."

I let my eyes drift closed and have the sudden sensation that I'm moving. I gasp and open them again, but I'm still sitting in the chair.

"You okay?" he asks.

I close my eyes again to see what happens. It feels like I'm climbing a roller coaster. "That's so weird. When I close my eyes I feel like I'm moving."

"That is weird," he says. "Do you know what I want?"

"No, what?"

He grins. "I don't know either. I was hoping you did."

We both erupt with laughter. I'm not sure why it's funny, but it's absolutely the most hilarious thing I've ever heard in my life. Our eyes meet across the table, and somehow *that's* funny. We're overtaken with a renewed bout of giggles.

"Man, I am high as fuck," Lucas says. "Those guys at the store didn't steer me wrong."

I can't seem to stop smiling. "Am I high as fuck too?"

Lucas doubles over with laughter. "Oh my god, Becca, I love it when you swear. It's like hearing a fucking Disney princess say a dirty word."

That makes me laugh again, and I cover my mouth to stifle the giggles. I have to be careful not to close my eyes for too long, or I feel like I'm going to fall over.

"Come on, let's go inside," he says. "I think we've had plenty."

We go in and stretch out on the couch, all smiles and laughs, and start talking about... who even knows. We talk about my apartment, the way the sand feels between your toes when you walk on the beach, and some weird TV show Lucas used to love but can't remember what it was called. There's an awareness in the back of my head that maybe I'm not making a lot of sense, but Lucas seems to understand every word. He nods and smiles, looking at me through half-lidded eyes, his hands behind his head.

My god, he's beautiful. His face is literally perfect, with this jawline that someone should paint because it's so gorgeous. Fucking gorgeous, let's just put it out there. He always has what looks like a couple days' growth of stubble, not much more, and it emphasizes the lines of his face without overwhelming his good looks. His eyes are this beautiful shade of hazel—sometimes they seem brown, other times green. And don't even get me started on his body. I don't want to admit how many times I've pictured him naked, wondering what he looks like under his shirt.

Or under his pants.

I think he just asked me a question, because he's looking at me with his eyebrows raised, like he's expecting an answer. I glance down at the bag of Doritos in my lap. It's half gone, and I have no memory of eating a single one. But my fingers are stained orange, and when I lick my lips, I taste the salty processed cheese flavor.

"What?"

"Can I have the chips?"

"Oh, right." I pass him the chips and he hands me an Oreo, and it's definitely not the first one I've eaten.

My head is sort of dreamy, and the edges of my vision are tinged with a misty haze. Lucas turns on a movie, but my mind is fuzzy, so it's hard to pay attention. We sit on opposite ends of the couch, our feet tangled together, passing food back and forth. This is a lot of touching for us, but I don't feel awkward about the way he keeps rubbing his toes against my feet. It's the most normal thing in the world.

Plastic crinkles, and I wake up with a start. I don't remember falling asleep, but Lucas takes the bag of gummy bears off my chest where it almost spilled, and puts it on the coffee table.

"Our movie is over. And you keep falling asleep," he says with a smile.

"Sorry," I say. "Am I still high?"

He laughs. "Yeah, we both are. It makes me sleepy too, after a while. I'm going to head home and crash. Do you want to go upstairs, or just stay here?"

I roll onto my side and close my eyes. It's way too much work to get up. Or answer his question.

A minute later, I feel a blanket settle over the top of me.

Lucas pulls it up to my chin and tucks it in around my body. His hand brushes against my face, moving my hair back.

"Night," he says, his voice soft.

"Goodnight," I mumble, but I think he's already gone.

## 11

# LUCAS

Gabe texts me mid-afternoon, letting me know that our regular Thursday pub night has been moved to Danny's Tavern. Apparently Finn wants a change of scenery. Can't say I blame him. He spends a lot of time at his pub—although less now that he's with Juliet, which is probably good for him.

I think about asking Becca if she wants to come, but I glance out my front window and don't see her car. Plus, the guys would probably give me shit if I bring her. It isn't so much that pub night—or tavern night, as it were—has to be guys only. Juliet has hung out with us on Thursday nights a few times, and it's cool. But Gabe and Finn have been giving me a hard time about hanging out with Becca so much. Last week they wouldn't stop drilling me with questions about her, like they were trying to get me to admit there's something going on between us that isn't.

Still, it's disappointing that she's not home. Maybe I'll text her later and see if she wants to come join us.

I head out around nine and find a spot in front of

Danny's. There are quite a few other cars here—kind of surprising for a Thursday, even in the summer. But the town has been packed this week. I'm surprised Finn and Gabe are both taking a night off.

Inside, most of the tables are taken, and the barstools are all full. I find Finn and Gabe sitting at a table, a couple of empties already in front of them. I veer toward the bar and get a beer before I join them.

"Hey." I sit down and take a swig. "What's up tonight?"

"Not much," Finn says. "The fucking stove went out at the pub, so I spent all day fixing it. I had to get out of there or I was going to punch someone."

I nod. "Fair enough."

"So what's up with you?" Gabe asks. "I'm surprised you came tonight."

"Why are you surprised?"

"I don't know," he says with a shrug. "Seems like you're always busy lately."

"Cute girl moves in next door..." Finn says.

"Fuck off, you two," I say. "Leave Becca alone."

"Speaking of," Gabe says, nodding toward the door.

I look over my shoulder and see Juliet and Becca come into the tavern. Becca's wearing a fitted blue top and short skirt, with a pair of sandals. She has her hair pulled up, showing off her neck. Our eyes meet and she gives me a little smile. Seeing her sends a pang of nervousness through me. That's weird. Why is she making me jittery? I take a long pull from my beer while she and Juliet walk over to our table.

"Hey," Juliet says. "Sorry, I figured you guys would be at the pub tonight. We won't intrude."

Finn stands and kisses her. "It's fine. You guys can hang out."

"No, no," she says. "You guys enjoy your beer and talk about man stuff. There's a table right over there. We're good."

Becca waves her fingers at me before she walks away with Juliet. It's stupid how disappointed I am that they don't stay.

Gabe raises his eyebrows at me.

"What?" I ask.

He shrugs. "Nothing. That was... interesting."

I ignore him. Finn and Gabe always give me shit about women. This isn't any different.

Finn starts talking about football, and I'm glad for the change of subject. I glance over and notice Becca sitting alone. Juliet's at the bar, probably ordering drinks. I need to quit watching Becca, but it's like I can feel her from across the room. Not to mention, her legs look fucking phenomenal in that skirt.

Looking around the crowded bar, I realize I'm not the only guy watching her. Some jackass in a sleeveless shirt and basketball shorts is eying her up and down like she's on display at a store. I have no reason to be pissed that some other guy is looking at her, but it makes my back tighten and I ball my hands into fists.

I try to pay attention to what Finn and Gabe are talking about, but I keep glancing at Becca. One of the bartenders comes to her table with a drink and puts it down in front of her. She looks confused, and he points to the douchey guy in basketball shorts.

Oh my god, he sent her a drink? What a cliché.

The guy saunters over to her table and slips into the chair across from her. *Way to sit with a girl without being invited, asshole.* Becca gives him a polite smile and they start talking. I notice she doesn't take a sip of the drink he sent her. It's probably something she hates.

Juliet comes back and sits down, but the guy doesn't get up. Finn starts casting glances at their table. Juliet smiles at him and shrugs her shoulders.

I go back to my beer and try to ignore the jackass hitting on Becca. She's a single woman; she can meet someone if she wants.

Although it pisses me off.

Eventually, he gets up and goes back to his friends. He says something to the other guys he's with, and nods, a smirk on his face. He looks at his phone. She didn't give him her number, did she?

Fuck.

With the guy away from Becca's table, I'm slightly less distracted. The three of us talk about work, and sports. Then Finn starts talking about wedding shit, and I check out of the conversation.

After a while, Becca and Juliet get up. Finn waves at Juliet, and the girls head for the door.

Of course the jackass follows them out.

Great. Now I have to decide what to do. Does Becca want that guy to follow her? Is he being a creeper, and she could use some help? I have no right to intervene, but the thought of her hooking up with him makes my blood boil. Becca wouldn't really take off with him, would she? It's not like she's alone. Juliet is out there.

Fuck it. I'll just go out and make sure she gets into Juliet's car.

"Be right back," I say to Finn and Gabe, and head outside.

I poke my head out the door and glance around. Becca is standing in the parking lot, talking to the guy. I don't see

Juliet anywhere. I hesitate for a beat. Where's Juliet? She wouldn't leave Becca standing there, would she?

The guy gets closer to Becca. She takes a step back and crosses her arms.

"Hey, Becca." I walk toward them. "You okay? Do you need a ride home or anything?"

She looks at me and her eyebrows draw together. "I'm fine. I'm going home with Juliet."

"All right, just making sure."

"Hey, man, the lady is fine," the guy says. "We're just having a little chat. You can back off."

Anger bursts through me, running hot in my veins. "Excuse me? You can *fuck* off."

"Lucas," Becca says.

"What, are you the ex-boyfriend or something?" the guy asks.

"No, he's not," Becca says. She shoots me a glare. "He's my neighbor, and he's going home."

I put my hands up. "Hey, I'm just making sure you're okay."

"I'm fine," she says, irritation plain in her voice. "I said that already."

Juliet pulls up in her car. Becca glares at me again as she walks to the passenger side.

"It was nice meeting you," Becca says to the guy. "Have a good night." She gets in Juliet's car without saying anything to me.

The dude scowls at me, like it's my fault Becca didn't leave with him. Thankfully, he doesn't say anything else—just goes back inside the bar. I stand in the parking lot like an idiot and watch Juliet and Becca drive away.

That was shitty.

I go inside long enough to say goodbye to the guys. I

don't tell them I made a jackass out of myself in the parking lot—just that I'm beat and ready to call it a night.

When I get home, I head straight for Becca's door, knowing full well it makes me a glutton for punishment. But I don't want her to be mad at me. I was only trying to look out for her.

Friends can do that, right?

She opens the door and rolls her eyes. "Really?"

"Can I come in?"

She turns and walks inside, leaving the door open. I follow.

"Becca, I'm sorry about what happened at the bar," I say. "I was just checking up on you."

She whirls on me. "That's the problem. I didn't need you to *check up* on me. I'm a grown woman, Lucas. If I want to talk to a guy at a bar, I'm more than entitled."

"Of course you are," I say. "That's not the point."

"Oh, it isn't?" she asks. "Then why were you glaring at him the entire time he was at my table?"

"I wasn't glaring."

She raises her eyebrows. "No? Then you must have had the... shittiest beer ever to make you scowl like that. And what was with following me outside?"

"I just wanted to make sure—"

"You thought I was going to leave with him, didn't you?"

I open my mouth to answer, but I'm pretty sure everything I say from this point forward is only going to dig me into a deeper hole.

"Seriously?" she asks. "First, I have better taste than that. Second, if I did leave with him, it's none of your business. And third, well, I have better taste than that."

"I just wanted to be sure you were all right."

"Damn it, Lucas," she says, putting her hands on her

hips. "I have enough people who think they always have to look out for me. I'm surprised my dad hasn't suggested I install a home surveillance system yet. And Juliet basically chased that guy away from our table, like I couldn't handle it. Granted, I wasn't interested, but it would be nice if everyone wouldn't assume I'm too helpless to take care of myself."

My shoulders slump. "I'm sorry, Becca. I didn't mean it like that."

"Then what did you mean?"

I look down. I can't tell her the truth—that seeing that guy talk to her made me jealous as fuck. That's idiotic. Becca isn't my girlfriend. I don't *want* a girlfriend.

"I don't know," I say. "I'm sorry."

She takes a deep breath. "It's okay. I know you were just trying to be nice. I'm just so tired of people stepping in to rescue me."

One corner of my mouth turns up in a grin. "Even from spiders?"

That gets a smile out of her. "That's different. I asked for your help."

"You're right, that's different." I step closer and hold out my arms. "I'm sorry about tonight. That was uncalled for. Forgive me?"

She gives me a shy glance and moves forward. "Yeah."

I wrap my arms around her and press her close, while she puts her arms around me. Oh, holy shit, this was a bad idea. Her floral scent fills me and her warm body feels amazing next to mine. I hold her for a few seconds longer than a *friend hug*, but I can't make myself let go.

I drop my arms and step back before I do something I shouldn't. "Well, as long as we're good, I should get home."

"Yeah, we're good." She sounds a little breathless.

"Night, Becca."

I leave her standing in the middle of her apartment. Every bit of me wants to turn around and kiss the fuck out of her.

But I can't.

## 12

# BECCA

Lucas appears at my back door, smiling at me through the glass. Whenever he does that, I'm hit with a mix of excitement and nervousness. Sometimes it means he has another one of his ideas. But a lot of the time, the two of us just hang out—nothing scary or naughty involved.

It hasn't escaped my notice that I spend a lot of time with Lucas. Most of my free time, in fact. I see him way more than Juliet, and she doesn't live all that far away.

But he lives next door, so it's easy. I like living alone, but I do get lonely. It's fun to have a friend close by. And I always cook too much, so why not share it with him? He certainly appreciates it.

Brandon never did.

Lucas's wide smile pushes thoughts of Brandon out of my mind in an instant.

"Hey, darling," he says when I open the door.

I smile at him. I don't know why he calls me *darling*, but I love it. I hope he never stops. "Hey. What's up?"

He comes in and sits down on the couch, putting one arm over the back cushions. "Nothing. You?"

I slowly lower myself down, but stay on the edge. He's up to something. I'm sure of it. "What are you doing?"

"What?" he asks, looking around with feigned innocence.

"I know that look."

He grins. "I have an idea."

"Oh, boy."

"Naughty side, right?"

I narrow my eyes at him. "I feel like anything I say right now is going to get me in trouble."

"Have you ever watched porn?"

"Oh, god." I feel like this is a pattern with us. He comes in, suggests something I've never done, and am probably terrified of doing. I tell him all the reasons I can't. He doesn't listen and keeps pushing until I agree. Maybe this time I should just skip the middle part and go with it. After all, it isn't like he's going to let me out of this.

"Fine," I say. "Let's watch porn."

He blinks at me with a look of surprise. "Really? Just like that?"

"Are you going to let me out of it if I say no?"

"No."

I shrug. "Then let's get this over with."

He laughs. "This is progress. A month ago, you would have argued with me for ten minutes."

I guess he's right. Maybe this *is* progress. I bite my lower lip, hesitating before I say it. "Well, just fuck it, I guess."

"Literally," he says, pointing a finger at me. "And that was awesome. Let's go over to my place though."

"Why? Do you have a collection?"

He wiggles his eyebrows at me. "What do you think?"

"Gross, Lucas."

He laughs. "No, but I don't think you need to watch an entire shitty porn flick to get the experience. We can just find something online, and all you have is your little laptop."

"Fine. Should I bring snacks?"

He looks at me for a second with a slightly open mouth. "You know what, why not? I guess we can eat popcorn while we watch people fucking."

I groan and put a hand over my eyes. "Why do I let you talk me into these things?"

"Because it's fun."

I raise my eyebrows at him. "Fun?"

He grins at me again. "It's fun for me."

We go out the back door and over to his place. He grabs a dining chair and moves it to his office area.

"You can have my chair," he says. "It's more comfortable."

I settle into his office chair, tucking my legs beneath me, and open the bag of popcorn.

"So, be honest," he says. "Have you ever watched porn?"

"No, I never have."

"Perfect." He starts typing. "We'll watch something really mild, okay? Nothing too kinky. In fact, let's go for cheesy." He scrolls through some things, and seems to find what he's looking for. "Oh yeah, this should be awful."

"Awful?"

"Yep, and I think it's short, so if you really hate it, it will be over quickly."

He brings up something on one of the screens, clicks play, and sits in the other chair. The credits begin, and it looks like the lowest of low budget movies ever made. It starts and we both laugh. The acting is terrible, but I guess that isn't the point.

"Do men actually find those enormous fake boobs attractive?" I ask.

"I guess," Lucas says. "It's not my thing, though."

I reach over and poke him. "Yeah, right. You're probably so turned on by her."

"Not so much," he says. "Oh wait, now it's going to get good. The copy machine repair guy showed up."

There's some more dialog, but mostly they just start taking their clothes off.

"Is that thing real?" I ask when the guy gets naked. His dick is huge.

"Yeah, probably," Lucas says.

"God, it's terrifying. I wouldn't let that guy anywhere near me."

Lucas laughs. "Come on, I thought women want dudes with huge dongs."

"Not that huge."

The couple start to go at it, and I hate to admit, but there's a little something about it that's arousing. Mostly it's ridiculous and kind of gross. But I'm feeling a little warm.

Okay, the truth is, it isn't the movie that's turning me on. I glance at Lucas from the corner of my eye. The lines of his face are illuminated by the glow of the screen. Watching this *with Lucas* is kind of a turn on. I shift in my chair and swallow hard, trying to ignore the tingly feeling between my legs.

It goes on for a while. They stop at one point, and I think maybe it's over, but after a few badly delivered lines of dialog, they start up again.

Another actor shows up on screen. I think he's supposed to be shocked, but he's taking his clothes off pretty fast, so I don't really get who he is or if there's a point to him being there.

"Uh-oh," Lucas says.

"What? Is that guy going to—"

The first guy gets the woman on her knees and starts ramming into her from behind, while the other stands in front of her and she puts his dick in her mouth.

"Ew," I say.

"Yeah, this is too much dick for me," Lucas says with a laugh. He hits stop and it freezes with the actress in a very unfortunate position. He closes the window quickly.

"So, is that it?" I ask.

"Why, do you want to watch more?"

"No," I say. "I'm just wondering if it's over. I feel like I need a shower."

Lucas laughs. "I think we're good. You watched porn. Do you feel naughty now?"

The way he says that, with one eyebrow raised and that smirk on his face, turns me on a hundred times more than watching people have sex on his computer screen.

I look away, hoping I'm not turning red. "Yeah, I guess so."

"Because if that was too tame, I can find something else—"

"No! I think I can cross porn off the list. I watched, and I didn't even close my eyes."

"That's true. I'm proud of you, darling." He gets up and goes into the kitchen. "You know, I think you're getting better at this stuff. You might be close to being end-of-*Grease* Sandy."

It shouldn't be disappointing to hear him say that, but it is. What happens when our little game is over? Will he still want to hang out with me all the time?

"Oh, I don't know," I say, trying to keep my tone casual. "I don't have the big hair yet, so..."

"True," he says. "Want a beer?"

"Sure."

I get up and we both move to his couch. We drink our beer and chat for a while. I try not to let my eyes drift down to his crotch, but I'm suddenly consumed with curiosity. What does he have under there? Does it look anything like the guy in the video?

I hope not.

Although, why do I *hope* anything when it comes to Lucas's man parts?

But I watch him as he sits, sipping his beer and talking with me, and the warm feeling in my core won't go away. I try to think of something else—force myself to stop thinking about Lucas naked—but nothing works. The more I try not to think about what he would look like behind me, grabbing my hips and thrusting himself into me, the more I can't get the picture out of my head.

I think watching a twenty-minute porno broke something in my brain. I've never been this consumed with thoughts of sex before.

I finish my beer and decide I need to get home. I say goodnight and go through the back door to my apartment.

I close the curtain and fall onto my couch. What is wrong with me? There's so much tension in my body. My pussy is literally throbbing.

There *is* something I could do to take care of it.

I glance around, feeling embarrassed already. But it's dark outside, and my curtains are closed. I live alone. The walls are thin, but I can stop myself from making noise.

And let's be honest—it would feel so good.

I take a deep breath and shift so I'm lying down on the couch. I slip my hand into my shorts and feel my panties.

They're soaked.

I find my clit and start to rub slowly, thinking about Lucas. The lines of his face. The set of his jaw. Those eyes. His hair. And that body. Oh my god, what a body he has. I imagine what it would look like, braced on top of me. His muscles straining, flexing. A sheen of sweat on his chest.

I bet Lucas is amazing in bed. He has the easy confidence of a man who knows what he's doing. What would it feel like, to have his mouth on my skin? His hips driving into me?

What would it feel like for Lucas to fuck me?

Fuck me.

Fuck.

I'm saying it in my head, but I'm pretty sure that's progress.

I rub harder, finding that a quick circular motion works best. I breathe hard as the tension builds. Yep, this is what I needed. I let go of my inhibitions, bit by bit, as if I'm loosening a chain that I keep wound tightly around myself. I explore my most tender places, letting my fingers seek out my sensitive bundle of nerves. I keep my eyes closed and let the world fall away.

Just a little more.

Right.

There.

*Bang, bang, bang.* There's a knock on my back door and I gasp, my eyes flying open.

I take a couple of quick breaths and fix my clothes. Oh god, my fingers are wet with... well, I don't want to think about what they're wet with. My face is absolutely on fire.

I run to the kitchen and wipe off my hand on a paper

towel. Looking down, I make sure my shorts aren't bunched up or anything, and smooth down my hair. I take a deep breath and open the door.

Lucas is standing on the back step, holding out my phone. "Hey, Becca, you left your—"

He stops mid-sentence, his eyes widening.

He can tell.

He *knows*.

I swallow hard, but I can't do anything except stare at him. I'm frozen in place, my feet rooted to the floor, my hand on the door handle.

"Sorry," he says, a grin stealing over his face. "Am I interrupting?"

Oh god. I'm breathing too hard and I know my face is redder than Lucas's shirt.

"No," I say, and my voice is too high pitched and breathy. "No, not at all."

"I, um..."

Even in the midst of my utter mortification, it's oddly satisfying to see Lucas a little frazzled. He's not sure what to say. I wonder if he...

*Don't look at his crotch, Becca. Don't do it.*

I look.

He's hard.

Oh god.

I spring into motion, desperate to end this horrifying moment. I grab my phone out of his hand and start closing the door.

"Thanks for bringing this back," I say.

Lucas puts his hand on the door, stopping me from closing it. "You sure you don't need help with anything?"

I freeze again. He did *not* just suggest what I think he suggested. I'm pretty sure my toes are blushing by now.

I try to stammer out a reply. "No. I'm not... I wasn't... I mean..." I shut the door in his face and the curtain falls, obscuring him from my view.

I stand there for a long moment, horrified. That was so rude of me. But he knew what I was doing. And he asked if I wanted *help*. I'm equal parts mortified and—dare I even admit—tempted.

I go back to the couch and sink down. I'm so embarrassed, I want to die right here. My phone buzzes with a text, and I can hardly bring myself to look at it. Of course it's from Lucas.

*Proud of you, darling.*

I cover my face, but I can't lie—I'm smiling.

I guess if I'm going to make him really proud, I should finish what I started.

## 13

# LUCAS

I grab the coffees from the counter and bring them over to our table. Becca is occupied with something on her phone, but she sets it down when I slide her coffee toward her.

"Thanks," she says with a smile.

The weather is colder than it's been recently, and she's wearing a light pink sweater over a white t-shirt, and jeans. She texted me this morning, saying she wanted to get out of the house, so we decided to go out for coffee.

Her phone vibrates and she rolls her eyes.

"Everything okay?" I ask.

She checks her phone and sets it down again. "Yeah, it's just my dad. He's trying to convince me to move home."

I stare at her for a few seconds too long, but hearing her say that is strangely alarming. "Why?"

She shrugs. "My parents didn't want me to move out here in the first place. They'd prefer it if I lived close. Or at their house."

"They really are overprotective, aren't they?" I ask.

"You have no idea. It's kind of silly. I guess it would be

worse if they didn't care about me, or were mean or something. But it drives me crazy. It's like they don't think I can handle anything on my own." She pauses and looks down at the table. "I know why they're like that, though."

"Why?"

"I had a sister."

Normally, I'm kind of a clueless guy, but there's no mistaking the grief in her voice. "Had?"

"Yeah, her name was Alicia. She died when I was eight. She was ten."

"Oh, shit, Becca. I'm sorry. What happened?"

"It was a car accident," she says, her eyes still on the table. "My dad was taking her to a piano lesson. It wasn't his fault, but I know he blames himself."

"So now he's trying to protect you from everything because he's afraid of losing you too."

She nods. "I think so. It's weird, because they never talk about her. They put all the pictures of her away and got rid of all her things. If you go to my parents' house, it's like she never existed. Although I know my mom kept some of her stuff, and they have a box of photos with her in them. But they never let people see any of it. Even me."

"That's awful." I take another sip of coffee because I'm not sure what to say. I'm not usually the guy people open up to.

"I'm sorry, I know it's uncomfortable to talk about stuff like this."

"No, it's okay. Your parents make more sense now."

"Yeah, I understand why they act the way they do," she says. "I just wish they'd let go a little. They keep trying to orchestrate my life so nothing bad ever happens to me. I was even with Brandon because of them."

Oh, shit. The ex. Since the first day we met, and I made

her cry by mentioning her ex-boyfriend, she's barely said a word about him. All I know is that she expected a ring, and got dumped instead, and that's why she moved out here.

I can't decide if I want to hear about him or not.

"What did your parents have to do with him?"

She takes a deep breath. "They're friends with his family; they attend all the same social events and stuff. Brandon's family is a lot like mine, I guess. My parents more or less hand-picked him for me. The first time I went out with him was on a date that was literally arranged by my parents."

I raise my eyebrows. "You're kidding."

"Nope," she says. "From that first date, my parents assumed I'd marry him. I guess I did too, even that early. It seemed like it was what everyone expected, so I went along with it. My parents weren't even mad when I moved in with him, although they're kind of old fashioned about that stuff. I think they wanted me to be with him because they thought he'd take care of me, the way they always did."

"You were their fragile little princess, and they wanted to make sure they passed you off to the right prince," I say.

She nods. "Yep, that was it. And the weird thing is, at the time, it all seemed to make sense. Of course I was with Brandon. Looking at us from the outside, we probably seemed perfect together. Like we were destined to get married."

I pause for a second, wondering if I should ask this question. "Did you want to marry him?"

"I thought so," she says. "We dated for a long time, and I pretended like I didn't care that he hadn't proposed. But the truth is, I started expecting a ring after about six months. My mom was one step away from planning our wedding already. Everyone around me seemed to think it was a given."

"But did you actually *want* to marry him?" I ask again.

She meets my eyes. "No. He would have kept me in a cage. I was just too scared to imagine my life outside that cage. Being with him seemed safe."

I grin at her. "A cage is no place for you, darling."

She laughs. "What about you? Have you always been like this?"

"Like what?"

"You know, perpetually single."

I rub the back of my neck. I don't like talking about this, but I have no reason to keep it from her. "No, I was with someone when I lived in New York. Valerie. I guess I thought the same thing you did—that I'd marry her."

Her mouth drops open. "Are you serious?"

"Yeah, is that surprising?"

She shrugs. "It is, actually. What happened with her?"

"She left me." I take a sip of my coffee. "Okay, she didn't just leave me. We were living together, and she started cheating on me with someone she worked with."

Becca covers her mouth with her hand and her brow furrows. "Oh my god, Lucas. That's horrible."

"It was. It sucked. She and I were kind of a disaster, though. Valerie had a big personality, and a temper. We fought a lot. Even if she hadn't cheated on me, I think we would have crashed and burned eventually. Besides, she didn't even stay with the guy she cheated with. I heard she broke up with him just a few months later."

"Is that why you moved back here?"

I shift in my chair. "Yeah. I felt like I needed to start over. Sometimes I wonder if coming here was the right thing, though. I could have had a fresh start somewhere else, and here I have to deal with my dad hounding me about taking over his store. But it's home."

"I'm sorry that happened to you," she says.

"Thanks," I say. "I'm sorry you got hurt too. Although you did say you threw up on him, so that's kind of awesome."

Her cheeks color a little and she laughs. "It was *not* awesome at the time. But looking back, I guess it's a funny story."

"It's a fantastic story."

She takes another sip of coffee. "Brandon wasn't all that great, anyway. He wasn't a jerk to me or anything. But you treat me better than he ever did, and we're not even, you know…"

It's enormously satisfying to hear her put me above her douchey ex—even though we're just friends.

"Was he at least good in bed?" I ask with a wink.

She shrugs. "I don't really know."

"You don't know?" I ask. "You were with him four years, and you guys weren't…"

"No, we were," she says. "But I don't have a lot to compare him to. I guess he was okay."

I raise my eyebrows. "If you're not sure, there's clearly something wrong. What was he good at?"

Her cheeks flush deeper. "What do you mean?"

"What did he do that was awesome?" I ask. "Like, was he really good with his tongue?"

"Um…" She stammers a little and hesitates. "Do you mean, was he good with his tongue in certain places?"

"Becca, you aren't going to get in trouble for saying it. Was he good at eating you out?"

She looks away. "I don't know because he never did that."

"Shut up."

"What?" she asks. "Is that weird?"

"Yeah, it's fucking weird," I say. "He never went downtown? Ever?"

"No."

I stare at her. She has to be kidding. Holy shit. "Is that because you didn't want him to? Or he wasn't into that?"

She looks away again. Her sweet flushed cheeks and nervous finger tapping against her coffee cup are so damn endearing. I know she's uncomfortable talking about this, but at the same time, she *is* talking about it. With me. It feels like I'm seeing a side of her she doesn't let anyone else see.

"He never brought it up," she says. "And I was too scared to ask. I've never had a guy do that."

"Never?"

"Come on, Lucas," she says.

"I'm sorry," I say. "I'm just surprised. So I guess that means sex with Brandon was pretty vanilla."

She laughs. "Yeah, I suppose it was. Although he probably assumed I wouldn't want to do anything new, so he never tried. I think that's part of why he left me."

"Hey, don't start blaming yourself," I say. "I know people look at you like you're a breakable piece of glass. But anyone who really knows you should know better. If Brandon was afraid to get dirty with you, it just shows that he didn't see the real you."

"Yeah?"

"Absolutely," I say. "Look at all the stuff we've done together. I bet Brandon wouldn't believe you watched porn, or smoked weed."

"No, he'd never believe it. I almost don't believe it."

"But you did," I say. "You just needed someone to help you feel brave enough. If Brandon didn't make you comfortable enough to get freaky, that's on him, not you. A good guy will bring out the best in his girl."

Becca stares at me for a long moment. I hold her gaze, unable to look away.

"Yeah, I guess you're right," she says.

We're both quiet as we finish our coffee. I shift in my chair and try to think of anything other than Becca and sex, but it isn't easy. It's a bummer her ex was so lame, but I'm not surprised. I meant what I said to her. She shouldn't blame herself if he didn't bring out the best in her. A good girl can have a bad side, but she won't let it out for just anyone. It's not Becca's fault Brandon wasn't the guy to do that for her.

In a way, I suppose *I'm* that guy for Becca. But I'm not sure how far I should let that go.

## 14

# BECCA

Lucas slides open the back door without knocking and strides in. I look up from my book.

"Becca, I've been thinking."

I raise my eyebrows. "About what?"

"I've given a lot of thought to this," he says. "Even before our conversation earlier, to be honest. And I know you're going to say no at first, but I think this is really important in your quest to become end-of-*Grease* Sandy."

"What are you talking about?"

"There are some things holding you back," he says. "I've shied away from addressing them, but we're reaching the limit of where we can go with this in other areas. Unless you want to start breaking the law, which, if that's the case, that's beyond what I can help you with."

"Obviously I don't want to do anything illegal," I say. "Did you just meet me?"

He grins. "No, no I didn't. But there's an entire realm of experiences we haven't explored yet, and honestly, I don't think we can continue unless we start."

I'm afraid to admit I know what he's hinting at. The thought tickles at the edges of my mind, tapping against that door I keep tightly shut. And locked. Especially when I'm with Lucas. But he's starting to say it, and if he does, I'm afraid that door is going to fling wide open.

"I don't... um—"

"I think I need to go down on you," he says.

My eyes widen and I clutch my book to my chest. I thought he was going to say he thinks we should make out or something. Go down on me?

"What? We can't do that," I say, scooting back into the corner of the couch, like I can hide from him. Those little taps on my locked door get louder. "What are you even talking about?"

He sits on the edge of the couch, his eyes intent on my face. "You've never had your pussy eaten out. That's a travesty. No woman should go this long without having a guy tongue-fuck her—especially a guy who knows what he's doing."

I can't believe he's saying this to me, right here, in my living room. My Mickey Mouse clock looks down on us, his eyes full of scathing judgment.

"But people don't... we can't just... we're not..."

"I know we're not." He scoots closer and puts his hand on my foot. "And that's the best part. I can show you things, and help break you out of your shell a little more, but there's nothing complicated. We like each other, right? We enjoy doing things together. We can do this without it being a big deal. Come on, have I steered you wrong yet?"

"Well, no. But..."

"I'm not saying we need to get all emotional about it. I'm saying you wanted to find your naughty side, and this is something I can do to help you find it."

"God, Lucas, you make it sound so clinical. You're saying you want to perform... oral sex on me, like it's no big deal. Doesn't that kind of thing need to have some, I don't know, desire attached to it? You can't just pull my pants down and do stuff."

His face goes still, his eyes so intense. He licks his lips and there's something in his expression I haven't seen before. At least, I haven't seen it looking at him straight on like this. I've noticed that look in his eyes, but only from the corners of my vision. When it was easy to brush it off as my imagination.

"You mean I need to be attracted to you," Lucas says, his voice low. "I need to *want* to do it."

I swallow hard. "Well, yeah."

He takes a deep breath and runs his hand up my shin. "That's not an issue, Becca. I definitely want to do it."

Oh god. He's touching my leg with his big hand, and telling me he wants to... do things with me. To me.

My face heats up and Lucas's grip on my leg tightens.

"Lucas, this is crazy," I say, but my voice is so tiny, there's no conviction. His tongue darts out again, wetting his lower lip, and I have to stop myself from clenching my thighs together.

"This doesn't have to change anything," he says. "We can keep hanging out like before."

*Doesn't have to change anything.* Right. This isn't Lucas asking me out. He's not saying he wants to date me, or be my boyfriend. This is just like our other adventures. It's a new experience for me. Nothing more.

Would there be any harm in that?

He moves in closer and puts his hands on my knees, then rubs his thumbs around in slow circles. I stare at him, unable to look away. Am I going to let him do this? Am I going to get... naked... in front of Lucas? And then let him put his mouth—

I stand up, putting my book on the coffee table, and walk to the sliding door. Every inch of my body wants this. I close my eyes for a second, and I can already feel his tongue. That tongue that I've looked at so many times and wondered what it would feel like. Now he's offering it to me. He's willing to just... go for it, and do something I've never done before. And I have no doubt he's good at it. He's probably amazing.

But this is crossing a line. Although, he doesn't seem to think so. He doesn't take sex seriously, but I've never had casual sex. Ever. I've only slept with guys I've been dating, and never right away.

That door in my mind is peeking open, tantalizing me with what's on the other side.

Lucas comes up behind me. He's almost silent, but I can feel his presence, and my back tingles at his nearness. I try to suppress the sudden rush of arousal, but it washes over my whole body, from my scalp to my toes, making every nerve fire in unison.

He takes my hair in his hands and starts gently pulling, sliding his fingers through the strands, like he's going to put it up in a ponytail. I stand, frozen, while he twists it up and holds it against the top of my head with one hand.

"I'm sorry," he says, his voice so soft. "I didn't do this right."

He keeps my hair up and leans in, placing his lips on the back of my neck. My knees almost buckle, but somehow I stay standing. He pulls away, the kiss leaving a firebrand on my skin.

Lucas just kissed me.

His other hand brushes down my back and whispers against my hip. He steps closer, so his body is right behind mine, his hand still holding my hair. He kisses my neck again, right where it meets my shoulder.

He puts his mouth next to my ear. "I won't do anything you don't want me to. If you say no, I'll go and I won't bring it up again. But right now, Becca, I'd love to have my mouth on you. I'd love to taste you. I think it would be fucking fantastic, and I can guarantee you'd love it too."

The air sucks from my lungs. I can't breathe. I put a hand on the door to steady myself and try to take a deep breath.

"What happens... I mean... is that all?" I ask. "What about you?"

He drags his stubbly jaw along the side of my neck and my eyes roll back in my head. "What about me?"

God, Lucas, why are you making me spell this out? "Well, if you do that... and then, I, um, finish. What happens then? What will you do?"

I feel his smile against my cheek. "I'll probably just go home and jerk off with the taste of you still in my mouth."

My eyes widen. "Holy shit."

He laughs, his breath tickling my skin. "Come on, darling. You've trusted me with things before. Trust me with this. Let me do this for you." He lets my hair fall and grabs my hips with both hands, his face still near my ear. "I want to."

His grip on my hips is tight, almost possessive. I feel like he's about to bend me at the waist, pull down my pants, and take me from behind. If he suggested it, I think I might let him.

I'm in big trouble.

He takes my hand and gently tugs. I swallow hard and let him lead me upstairs to my bedroom. Somehow, I find myself on my bed, lying on my back, still dressed. Lucas kneels in front of me, his eyes dark with intensity. He unbuttons my jeans and lowers the zipper. I lift my hips so he can slide them off my legs.

He runs his hands up the outsides of my thighs. "Have I ever mentioned you have an incredible body?"

I can't help but smile at that. "No."

"You really do," he says. "I've been holding a lot back from you. But I think maybe I can let some of it out."

"Holding what back?"

"How sexy you are. And all the things I'd like to do to you."

I let out a nervous laugh, but my head is spinning. He's been thinking about this? Looking at me this way? Since when?

"I didn't think..." I'm having a hard time finishing sentences. But it's difficult when Lucas rubs his hands on my bare thighs. "I didn't think you were attracted to me."

His eyebrows lift. "You're kidding."

"No," I say. "I know you like me, and we're friends. But I sort of thought you saw me like a dorky little sister."

His mouth turns up in a smile. "You are the most adorable creature on this planet, do you know that? Every time I think I have you figured out, you say something crazy and I realize I have no idea how to handle you."

"I'm not crazy."

He climbs on top of me, nudging my thighs apart with his knee, and settles down so our faces are close. "You're crazy if you think I see you like a little sister."

"I just figured, you really like women," I say. "And you've never been like that—like *this*—with me."

"I know," he says. "Like I said, I've been holding back."

I'm absolutely talking too much, and probably stalling, but I also need to know. "Why have you been holding back?"

He brushes his nose against mine and licks his lips. "Mostly because you live next door. I know what tends to happen when I'm with a woman. I'm never in it for a relationship, and even when I make that clear, it sometimes gets complicated. And by that, I mean they end up hating me and wanting me dead. I didn't want that with you, especially when we'd still have to see each other all the time."

"And you don't think this will be complicated?" I ask.

"No," he says. "We both know what we're doing. But honestly, Becca, if you think it *will* be too complicated, we don't have to."

I don't know if he does it on purpose, but right as he says *we don't have to*, he shifts his hips a little, and I feel his erection grind into me. His cock is rock solid, and he's sitting in just the right spot.

I gasp and swallow hard. "I think it'll be okay."

He smiles. "Yeah, I think so too."

He lifts up and his hand goes for the waistband of my panties.

"Wait."

His eyes come to mine and he raises his eyebrows.

"Should we maybe, um, kiss first?" I ask. "It feels kind of weird to bypass kissing completely and go straight to, well..."

Lucas smiles and lowers himself back down. Oh my god, his cock is so hard. Is it hard for *me*? This is crazy.

"I'd love to kiss you," he says. "I wasn't sure if you'd want me to."

"You're about to have your mouth... you know. Plain old kissing is nothing compared to that."

He laughs and his whole body reverberates with it. "I'm about to have my mouth where?"

"Stop."

"No, I want to hear you say it," he says. "Then I'll kiss your mouth."

"You're holding my mouth kiss hostage?"

"Absolutely."

I roll my eyes. "What am I supposed to say?"

His eyes sparkle with mischief. "I want you to say, *Lucas, please eat out my pussy*."

I push against his chest. "No!"

He laughs again and thrusts his hips against me. Oh, for the love of everything that feels good…

"Come on, say it."

I squeeze my eyes shut. "Lucas, please eat out my pussy."

He makes a low noise in his throat and brings his mouth down onto mine. He's gentle at first, kissing my upper lip, then my lower. Tentatively, I put my arms around his back. He plants his lips harder against mine and his mouth starts to move. His lips are every bit as warm and soft as I thought they would be.

Holy shit, I'm kissing Lucas.

With my pants off.

His tongue brushes against my lips and I suck in a hard breath. I open for him, and his tongue surges in. It slides against the length of mine, like he's licking ice cream. Our tongues caress each other, and this is not a *plain old kiss*. This is a kiss unlike anything I've ever felt before. He's not just kissing me with his lips, he's kissing me with his whole body. His cock grinds into me through our clothes, one hand reaches down and squeezes my ass, and his weight on me makes me want him to do a lot more than kiss me, no matter how good he is at it.

And oh my god, he is *so* good at it.

He slides his tongue in and out of my mouth, hinting at what's to come. In no time, I'm kissing him back and rolling my hips against his erection. We both start to move, thrusting, grinding, rubbing against each other. He grabs one of my thighs and pulls it up higher. This is not turning out how we meant it to, but there's no part of me that cares. Hot fire races through my veins. Every bit of skin that touches Lucas wants more of it. More of him. All of him.

I grab his shirt and pull it up, desperately trying to get him undressed. He reaches over his shoulder, his mouth hardly leaving mine, and yanks the shirt over his head. I run my hands along his chest and shoulders, around to his back. All that hard muscle flexes over me. He kisses me again and grinds his cock against me. Without even thinking about what I'm doing, I slide my hands between us and try to unfasten his pants.

"Whoa, darling," he says, pulling away just enough that I can't reach his cock. He's breathing hard and his lips are red and full. "We're getting a little carried away."

"That's fine."

He looks me in the eyes. "Damn it, Becca, I could fuck you so hard right now."

My hands are on his arms and I dig my fingers into his biceps. "Okay."

He stares at me for another moment before moving back and practically ripping my panties off. Without any of his earlier gentleness, he pushes my knees open and buries his face between my legs.

He growls as he clamps his mouth on me and I feel his tongue move up my center. I don't know what I was expecting, but it wasn't this. My back arches and I let out a squeal, but before I can think about how lame that sounded, my eyes are rolling back in my head.

He explores with his tongue for a moment, running it up one side, then the other. He licks the center again and I cry out when he finds my clit. He teases it, first circling, then flicking it.

"Oh my god, Lucas, are you serious?"

His only response is to lick me harder, pressing against my clit with the flat of his tongue. I grip the sheets and close my eyes. His mouth is hot, his tongue so wet, and the way he's using it is literally blowing my mind. I can't even think.

He pushes his tongue inside my pussy and I groan. I usually try to stay quiet, but it's like I'm losing control of myself. His tongue moves in and out, dragging over my hot bundle of nerves in a steady rhythm. I move with him, rolling my hips against his mouth. I've never felt anything like it.

Lucas sucks a little, and varies the pressure. He speeds up, and my body moves of its own accord. The intensity builds and I'm panting, grabbing the sheets, writhing beneath him. He doesn't let up, the precise movements of his tongue driving me absolutely insane.

"Yes. Oh, god, Lucas. Yes, just like that. Oh my—"

Before I know what's happening, I'm coming. My core muscles clench and release, sending tingles and sparks through my whole body. My fingers tear at the sheets and I can barely breathe. Lucas lets out a long groan, his tongue still plunging into me as I come.

The climax subsides, and I can't even open my eyes. Lucas kisses my inner thighs a few times, his hands still gripping my legs.

I open my eyes and lift my head to look at him. He's

staring at me, his face flushed, his chin glistening wet. For a second, I think he's going to rip his pants off, climb on top of me, and give me his cock.

But he doesn't. He makes a noise in the back of his throat, gets up, and practically flies out of the room.

## 15

# LUCAS

I crash through my apartment door and slam it shut behind me. I can barely see straight, but I struggle up the stairs. Bathroom. The bathroom works.

The taste of Becca is all over my face—on my lips, in my mouth, on my tongue. Holy shit, she tasted like motherfucking honey. Better than honey. Her pussy was like this magical fucking fairy tale. I wanted to slam my cock into her so bad. I was half a second away from doing it—especially because I know she would have let me. She said yes before I started eating her out.

So why didn't I just do it?

I lotion up and lean one hand against the wall while I rub my dick like a fucking maniac with the other. I close my eyes, lick the taste of her off my lips, and I'm coming about two seconds later.

*Holy shit.*

The orgasm relieves the worst of the tension, but I still have a mild ache in my balls.

Maybe I shouldn't have kissed her like that. I didn't mean for it to turn into us dry humping each other on her bed. But once our mouths got going, our bodies followed. We couldn't help ourselves. As many times as I've fantasized about pinning her beneath me like that, the reality was better. Just kissing her was fantastic. She has this almost virginal air to her, but she kisses like a goddamn slut. And I mean that in the absolute best way possible.

Her hands made a bid to take my pants off, and warning bells went off in my head. I was about to lose myself and just fuck her already, but there was that little voice, telling me not to. When I decided to ask her if I could go down on her, I told myself I could only do it if I drew a hard line in the sand. That's the only way this would work. It had to be like our other experiments—just friends, having fun, doing something a little crazy. Letting myself go beyond that would mean I'd run the risk of ruining things between us. And I don't want to do that.

Yeah, I'm going to end up fucking Becca, probably in every way I can. I know this now, and it's stupid for me to deny it. But when I do, it's going to be after we've discussed it and agreed to it. It can't be because we start making out and lose control of ourselves.

That's when things get complicated.

Becca and I don't need complicated. We're kind of awesome together, as friends, and I'm pretty sure I can keep a handle on this as we explore a new side to our friendship. I can do this for her. I can help loosen her up and give her experiences she's never had before. Pretending like that wouldn't cross into fucking is just dumb. Of course it was always going to. Deep down, I knew that from the start.

I just have to make sure not to let it get weird.

I go to the sink and rinse off. I need to go back over there and talk to her. I left so abruptly, I don't want her to think something is wrong. And this next interaction we have—

this next moment—is going to tell me everything I need to know about whether I just fucked up royally, or opened a new door for us that we're both going to love walking through.

After cleaning up and putting on a shirt, I go back to her place. I knock a few times, but slide open the door and poke my head through without waiting for her to answer.

"Becca?"

She's on the couch, dressed, with a pink throw pillow in her lap. Her eyebrows lift and she bites her lower lip.

I come in and I can't keep the grin off my face. To my vast relief, she smiles back.

She tosses my t-shirt at me. "You left so fast you forgot your shirt."

I grab it midair. "Thanks. And, sorry about that. I had to go take care of something."

"That didn't take you very long."

I laugh and sit down on the couch. So far, so good. "Yeah, well, that's what happens when I tongue fuck a woman with a magical pussy. Finishing was easy."

She giggles and moves the pillow up, like she's going to play shy and hide behind it. "I can't believe you just said that."

"What I *said* is what you can't believe?"

She laughs again. Her face is flushed and her lips full. "Okay, what you did was..."

"It was what?"

I expect her to look away—she doesn't look me in the eyes when she's saying something that's hard for her to get out—but she holds my gaze. "It was amazing."

That's a nice boost to my ego. Fuck yeah, it was amazing. "Awesome. So, you're saying you liked it?"

She laughs again. "I would have thought that was obvious while you were doing it."

*Doesn't mean I don't want you to say it.* "Well, yeah, you seemed to be enjoying yourself. I just want to make sure."

"Lucas, that was the best orgasm I've ever had in my entire life."

I'm not bragging when I say she isn't the first woman to say that to me. But the fact that it's *Becca* saying that to me? It feels like I just won a million dollars.

"Look at you, talking about your orgasms," I say. "See, I told you this would be good for you."

She laughs and I'm flooded with relief. It isn't weird. Sure, she's acting a little demure, but that's just Becca. We're hanging out, like normal.

This was such an awesome idea.

"Okay, so tell me this." I scoot a little closer to her. "Do you want to stop there? Or do you want more?"

She raises her eyebrows again. "More of what we just did?"

"Yeah, that. But, maybe other things too?"

"So, you're asking me if I want to start doing things with you," she says. "Sexually."

I shift a little closer and put my hand on her foot. I feel like I need to be touching her to have this conversation. "I'm going to be totally honest with you right now. I don't do the girlfriend/boyfriend thing. You know that about me already, but I want to make it clear what we're talking about here. Being friends with you is awesome. We have fun, and I like hanging out with you. I also loved eating you out, and I'll do that for you as often as you want. I'd also really like to do other things with you. I have a feeling there's a whole world of sexual experiences you haven't had, and I'd love to be the one to give them to you. If you want that, I'm in. If that's too much for you, though, it's fine. No hard feelings, and we can just watch Netflix tonight or whatever."

Becca grins. "Is this what *friends with benefits* means? Like, we're friends, and we're not dating each other. But we have sex on the side?"

"Yeah, I guess that's what it would be."

She pauses for a moment, pressing her lips together. "There's one thing I need if we do this."

"What's that?"

"I have a feeling this could be a deal breaker, but hear me out." She takes a deep breath. "I can't sleep with you, or even just fool around with you, if you're sleeping with other women too."

"Deal," I say, surprising myself with how fast I answer.

"You didn't even think about it."

I smile and squeeze her foot. Come to think of it, I haven't slept with anyone else since I started hanging out with Becca. That's weird. "Didn't have to. That's totally fair. But if that's the case, I need the same thing from you."

"Oh right, like that would even be an issue," she says.

"Hey, you never know. You might meet some guy you want to fuck more than me." I throw my head back and fake laugh. "Right, that would never happen."

She laughs and throws the pillow at me.

"Okay, so our little adventure made me hungry," I say. "I think I'll go grab takeout somewhere. Do you want anything?"

She eyes me for a long moment, like this is a big decision she needs to make. "You know what? I'm good. I have some leftovers I'll heat up. But maybe I'll catch you later."

I grin at her. I totally see what she's doing. She's showing me she isn't suddenly attached to me just because I gave her an epic orgasm. This is her way of telling me we're good.

"All right, darling." I get up and wink at her. "I'll see you later."

I walk out of her apartment, telling myself I'm not bummed that she didn't want to hang out more. That was totally the right call. Keep things casual.

I also ignore the voice in my head that says what we just agreed to—being friends, hanging out, having sex, and not seeing other people—sounds a lot like we just agreed to be in a relationship. Because it isn't. There's a difference here, and we both know it. We acknowledged it, and it's good.

Becca isn't my girlfriend. I can't do that again. I can do anything she wants physically. I'll destroy her body every night if she wants me to. But beyond that? I can't go there. I'd have to open myself up to being hurt again, and it just isn't going to happen.

# 16

# LUCAS

I knock on Becca's back door and glance through the glass. I don't see her inside, but I think she's home. Her car is out front, at least. We don't have plans to hang out, but I haven't seen much of her for the last couple days.

I'm not sure if I want to admit this, but I miss her.

That thought makes me second guess coming over, but she comes downstairs and sees me through the sliding glass door. Her face lights up with a smile and she gives me a little wave.

She slides the door open. "Hey."

"Hey." I lift the bag of kettle corn I brought with me. I happen to know it's her favorite movie watching snack. "Busy tonight? I brought snacks."

"Well, when you bring kettle corn, how can I refuse?" She steps back. "Come on in."

I close the door behind me and set the bag on the coffee table. She brings a big bowl from the kitchen and I empty the popcorn into it.

"Should we watch a movie?" I ask.

She sits down in the center of the couch. "Sure."

I lower myself next to her and get a whiff of her perfume. God, she smells good—so light and feminine. She grabs the remote and turns on the TV, but I don't take my eyes off her.

"What sounds good?" she asks. "Have you seen this one?"

I tear my eyes away from her and glance at the screen. "Whatever you want is fine."

She puts down the remote and starts to reach for the bowl of popcorn, but pauses, her arm outstretched.

"What?" she asks.

"I don't know, what?"

"You're staring at me."

There's no point denying it. I *am* staring at her. Her shorts show off her fabulous legs and I can see bits of her white bra peeking out from beneath her blue tank top. Her hair is up in a messy bun with little tendrils hanging around her neck.

Ever since I went down on her the other day, I've been thinking about how she felt. How she tasted. How much I want more.

"Sorry," I say. "You just look really good."

She scrunches up her nose. "I'm a mess today."

I shift so I'm facing her and put my hand on her thigh to see how she reacts. "I guess I like you messy."

She gasps, but doesn't pull away. I slide my hand up her leg, feeling her soft skin. Her cheeks flush and she looks up at me through her eyelashes.

"Tell me something," I say. "Has anyone ever fucked you on this couch?"

"No."

"Do you want to change that?"

"For real this time?" she asks.

I pull her into my lap so her legs straddle me and slip my hands into her shorts, grabbing her ass. "For real this time. If you want to, that is."

"Yeah, I think I want to."

I draw her closer and her mouth comes to mine. She threads her arms around my neck and sinks into my kiss. Her lips are full and soft, and she tastes faintly of mint. I squeeze her ass, pulling her into me so she rubs against my erection.

She leans back and bites her bottom lip. She grabs my shirt and I help her pull it off, tossing it to the side. I lift hers over her head and reach around to unclasp her bra. She tenses up, so I slowly slide the straps off her shoulders. Her bra falls, revealing her beautiful small round tits.

"Oh my god, Becca." I can't take my eyes off her hard pink nipples. "You are so fucking sexy."

She giggles and brushes a strand of hair off her forehead. Tentatively, she trails her fingers down my chest and abs, pausing at the waistband of my sweats.

"Go ahead." I take her hand and put it on my cock.

She gasps and rubs up and down a few times, then squeezes me through my pants. I groan and run my hands up her ribcage and cup her breasts. I lean forward and take one in my mouth, caressing her nipple with my tongue.

"Oh, Lucas," she whispers.

I suck harder and she leans her head back, a whimper escaping her lips. She shifts her hips so her pussy rubs against my cock. I put my hands in her shorts again and I'm in fucking heaven—my hands all over her ass and her tits in my mouth. I kiss and suck and lick her until she's breathing hard and grinding against me.

I put my thumbs in the waistband of her shorts and she

moves so I can take them off. She settles back on my lap and plunges her hand into my pants.

Her eyes widen. She pulls my cock out and stares at it. "Oh my god, Lucas. You're..."

"I'm what?"

"You're really big," she says. "I'm not sure if I can, well..."

"You'll be fine, darling," I say. "We'll just take it slow."

She nibbles on her bottom lip again and slides her hand up and down the shaft. Her delicate hand looks fabulous wrapped around my dick like that. She lets go and moves off my lap, helping me undress. But instead of getting back on my lap, she kneels in front of me, her hands on my thighs.

Her tongue sweeps across her lips. "What if I, um..."

I lift my eyebrows in surprise. I was not expecting this. "If you want to, I certainly won't say no."

She grabs my cock at the base and leans forward, her eyes lifted toward mine. "I really want to."

I stare at her as she brings my cock to her mouth. Her tongue swirls around the tip a few times, and she gets me good and wet. The feel of her tongue gliding across my dick is extraordinary. I'm starting to breathe harder already and she's barely started.

She pulls the tip into her mouth, wrapping her lips around the shaft, and looks me straight in the eyes. It's the sexiest fucking thing I've ever seen in my life. She doesn't let go of my gaze while she slowly draws more of me into her mouth.

"Holy shit, Becca."

I grab the back of the couch as she starts to move. She slides my cock in and out of her mouth; I can't take my eyes off her. She can't fit me all in, but she uses her hand on the base, stroking me in time with the movement of her mouth.

I have no idea if she's ever done this before, but she's fucking brilliant at it.

She moves faster and I groan. The pressure builds, and I move my hips to thrust in her mouth a little harder. She moans, like she's enjoying this too, and there's nothing hotter than that.

I lose myself in the feel of her mouth. It's warm, and wet, and I slide in and out, rubbing up against the top of her mouth, to the back of her throat. I can't stop watching her. This gorgeous woman has my cock in her mouth, and that is something I did not think would ever happen.

"Fuck, this is so good."

She takes me in deeper and I run my fingers through her hair. She moans again, like she's never tasted anything better than me. This is the hottest blowjob I've ever had. She slows down, caressing me with her tongue, then plunges down on me, hard.

"Oh, fuck."

She pulls back, sucks on the tip, and slides me in again. Over, and over. My mind goes blank. I'm racing toward my climax, every movement of her sweet, hot mouth bringing me closer.

This feels so fucking good, but I don't know if she wants me to come in her mouth. "Becca, I'm so close. I'm gonna come unless—"

She picks up the pace and I can't think. I grab the couch, like I need to hang on for dear life. My balls tighten, my back stiffens, and I start coming.

"Oh fuck, Becca. Fuck, yes."

Her hands clutch my legs and I thrust into her a few times while my cock throbs. It's so intense, the rush washing over me, leaving me dazed.

Becca pulls away and I give her a second before drawing

her into my lap. I wrap my arms around her, and hold her body close.

"Fucking hell, Becca," I say into her neck. "That was mind-blowing."

She laughs softly and moves back so she can look at me. "You liked it?"

"That was unreal." I put my hand on the side of her face and lean in to kiss her, but she shies away.

"Are you sure you want to do that?" she asks.

I slide my hand around to the back of her neck and hold her in a tight grip. A guy who won't kiss a woman after she's given him a blow job is a straight-up asshole, as far as I'm concerned. "Come here."

I kiss her mouth, gently at first, teasing her lips apart with my tongue. She opens for me, and I slide my tongue into her mouth—that brilliant fucking mouth. I enjoy every inch of it—the feel of her lips, her tongue against mine. She's delicious.

She rubs against me, and I can already feel how wet she is. I slide my hand between her legs and gently slip two fingers inside her. She gasps and starts to move her hips as I rub against her clit.

"Just give me a second, darling, and I'll be ready for you."

"What?" she asks. "But you already…"

I kiss her again and grin. "I told you I'm fucking you on this couch. That was a promise."

My dick doesn't fail me, and after a few minutes, I'm hard again. Although I had no doubt—especially with a woman as exquisite as Becca, naked and straddling me, her pussy so wet I can barely control myself. I roll her onto her back and reach over to get a condom out of my pants pocket.

Becca laughs. "Do you always carry one of those with you?"

"No, but I figured I should bring one tonight, just in case."

"It's a good thing," she says.

I roll on the condom, then settle between her legs, my cock just outside her opening. Her body tenses up, so I kiss her again and only slide in the tip.

"Relax, baby."

Becca meets my gaze and nods while I push into her, slowly, carefully. I feel her stretch open around me. Her eyes flutter closed and a soft sigh escapes her lips.

"Oh, Lucas."

Her pussy is exquisite—so hot and tight. I slide into her until she sheathes me completely. "Holy fuck, Becca."

She opens her eyes, but they're glassy and unfocused. "What?"

"You feel incredible."

"I do?"

"Are you kidding?" I move in and out a few times, gently at first. Then I thrust all the way in and hold there. "How does that feel?"

"Amazing," she says, her voice soft. "You don't even have to move and it's the best thing I've ever felt in my life."

She is *so* good for my ego. I move faster and her body responds. She moves her hips, taking me in deeper. She starts to moan softly, but closes her mouth, like she's trying to stop herself.

I pause and run my thumb across her lips. "You can let go, Becca. No one is around to hear you but me."

"I'm used to being quiet," she says.

"Don't be, darling." I plunge in, harder this time. "I want to hear you."

I thrust again, in and out, picking up the pace, and her body moves with mine. She stays quiet at first, but it doesn't take long before her moans grow louder. I love feeling her let go, hearing the sound of her restraint fall away.

With my cock still inside her, I sit back on my knees and pull her toward me by her hips. I grab her thighs and hold her legs up, marveling at this beautiful woman as I drive myself into her. I take one of her hands and guide her fingers to her clit.

"Touch yourself here."

She hesitates for a second, but I thrust into her again and her eyes roll back. I get her fingers going and soon she's rubbing herself while I pound her.

"Oh god, Becca, that is so fucking hot." She looks fantastic, lying before me with her gorgeous tits, her legs in the air, fingering herself while I pound her. Her pussy heats up, clenching around me, and I know she's close. "Do you want to come like this? Or do you want something else?"

Her eyes focus on me and her hand pauses on her clit. "I have choices?"

"Anything you want, darling."

She stares at me for a second, her lips parted, her cheeks flushed. "Will you kiss me while you make me come?"

"Done." I lower myself down, shifting her legs so they wrap around my waist, and kiss her. I fuck her harder while my tongue caresses hers. She grips my back, her fingers digging in as she gets closer. I hold myself up with one hand and grab her ass with the other, keeping a steady rhythm that brings us both to the brink.

She pulls her mouth from mine as she loses control, calling out with the pulses of her orgasm. I grind into her, growling into her neck while she comes. Oh fuck, that feels so good. I wait until she slows down and drive into her, plowing her into the couch cushions. She heats up again and I know I have her. If I can hold off just enough, I think I can make her come again.

Multiple orgasms in three...

Two...

One...

"Holy fuck!" she cries out, and claws down my back.

I explode into her, releasing all that tension in an orgasm that shatters me. I break apart into a million pieces. Becca's skin, her scent, her pussy holding tight around my cock; it's everything. I thrust and groan and get lost in the sensation.

When my climax subsides, I stay on top of her for a long moment, catching my breath. It takes a few seconds for my brain to catch up. That was probably the best sex I've ever had. It was stunning.

I won't lie. It freaks me out a little bit.

Becca looks at me with a hopeful smile. I grin back, but resist the urge to kiss her again. I need to be careful with her.

"Wow," I say, a little breathless, as I get up off her. I turn and pull off the condom while she sits up.

"Yeah, wow." She brushes her hair back from her face and grabs her clothes off the floor. "I'll be right back."

She goes into the bathroom and I take a moment to get my shit together. I get my clothes back on and run a hand through my hair. I sink down onto the couch, my heart still pounding.

Becca comes out and smiles at me. Her cheeks are flushed, and her hair is still a little messy. She sits down on the couch next to me, and grabs the popcorn bowl, pulling it into her lap.

"Well, that was amazing," she says. "You still up for a movie?"

I laugh and grab a handful of popcorn. "Sounds good to me."

She grins again and gets the remote. I settle back into the couch and enjoy my post-sex euphoria. This thing with Becca is even better than I thought it was going to be.

## 17

# LUCAS

"I can't believe I let you talk me into this," Becca says.

She's sitting in the front seat of my car, dressed in a black tank top and shorts, her hair pulled up in a ponytail. She wrings her hands together in her lap and casts nervous glances in my direction.

"Of all the things I've talked you into doing, *this* is the one you can't believe?"

We're driving up the highway, heading north. I finally talked Becca into going surfing.

She looks at me out of the corner of her eye. "Of all the things we've done, this is the only one that potentially involves large predatory animals."

I laugh. "There aren't any sharks around here."

"Do you know that for sure?" she asks. "Because there could be. Or there could be other things that might mistake me for dinner."

I put my hand on her leg and squeeze her thigh. "You'll be fine. We won't see any sharks."

"Yeah, you don't see them until they bite you."

I shake my head and keep driving. The best surfing spots are north of Jetty Beach, and I packed a bunch of food and beer for afterward. I rented a surfboard and wetsuit for Becca and had my car loaded before I told her what we were doing. I knew it was going to be a challenge to convince her, so I wanted to make sure we'd be ready to head out as soon as I got the tiniest *yes* out of her. It took some work to get her to agree, but when she relented, I rushed her into my car and we headed toward the highway.

My favorite surfing spot is just past Gabe's restaurant. We pull out onto the gravel road leading to the beach and park along the side. The weather is a little cold for a day in the water, but that means there isn't anyone else out here, which is perfect. And once we get moving, we'll warm up just fine.

I turn off the car, but Becca doesn't unbuckle her seatbelt.

"Lucas, I really don't know if I can do this. I think I'm more scared of the ocean than spiders."

"I don't think it's possible to be more scared of anything than you are of spiders." I squeeze her leg again. "You can do this. I promise you can. Imagine how amazing it's going to feel."

She puts a hand over mine. "You won't get too far away from me, will you?"

I shift in my seat and touch her chin, turning her face toward me. "I'll be with you the whole time."

"What if I can't do it?"

"You can," I say. "We'll take it slow. Just one step at a time. I'll be right there."

There's still fear behind her eyes, but her back straightens and she nods.

We get out of the car and she strips down to a bikini. It

doesn't matter how many times I see her naked (and lately that's pretty often), I still love looking at her body. She's slender without being too skinny, with toned legs from all the running she does. I help her get into her wetsuit, then change into mine.

I get down both surfboards. Becca's is big, but a larger board is good for a beginner. She handles it like a champ, hauling it down toward the surf. I don't ask if she wants help with it; sometimes I can tell when she wants to prove she can do something herself.

"Okay, first we're just going to go out far enough that the water is about hip deep on you. The waves won't be high there, and you can get used to being in the water."

She chews on her bottom lip, but nods. We walk out into the water. It's so cold, it's painful at first, but it doesn't take long before our feet get numb. The wetsuits keep the rest of our bodies warm enough, and we wade out until the water hits the top of Becca's thighs and the waves carry up past her waist when they roll by.

Our surfboards float next to us. Becca holds hers like it's the only thing keeping her from being swept out to sea.

"See, this isn't so bad," I say.

"This is terrifying."

A larger wave rolls past, coming up to her chest, and she gasps.

"You've got this, darling," I say, my voice firm. "You can do this."

I have her lean on her surfboard and pick up her feet to see how it feels when the waves move her. At first she jumps off immediately. But after a few tries, she's able to stay on and move up and down with the water.

"Okay, it's time to get on and paddle out farther."

She gets a little groove between her eyebrows, and I can

practically feel her fear, but she nods. I show her how to get on the surfboard, on her stomach so she can reach down and paddle with her arms.

"Don't go too far," she says.

"I won't. Trust me, Becca."

We move out, close to where the waves are breaking. I explain how to point the board toward the beach and paddle to get going when a wave is coming.

"You can even stay on your stomach, just like you are. We'll work on standing up later."

We move out farther and turn around so we're facing the beach. The first wave comes, but she doesn't get going fast enough. It rolls beneath her. We try a few more times, but catching your first wave is tricky.

"I don't know what I'm doing wrong," she says after missing another wave.

"You need to stop holding back," I say. "Let go and own it."

She wipes a few strands of hair off her face and looks at me with fierce determination in her eyes. Another wave comes behind us and we both start paddling.

"That's it, Becca," I yell at her as the wave starts to crest. "Keep going!"

The wave catches beneath her and instead of rolling over the top of it, she rides the crest. She picks up speed and grabs the sides of the surfboard. I catch the same wave and ride it in with her.

We both lose momentum as we get closer to the beach, although we're still in deep water. Becca looks back at me over her shoulder, her eyes lit up.

"Did I do it?"

"Becca! You did it!"

I paddle toward her, grinning like an idiot. I'm so proud

of her. She spins around so she's facing me, and her smile lights up the world.

"Oh my god! I did it!"

I laugh and jump down, intending to grab her and hug the shit out of her. But my board pops out of the water and flies at Becca.

It hits her right in the fucking head.

The whole thing happens in slow motion, but I'm moving the slowest of all. My board glances off her temple and she brings a hand up to her head. Her eyes close and she tilts to the side, slipping into the water.

I lose sight of her and panic grips me. Another wave rolls past and she doesn't come up.

"Fuck!"

I dive beneath the surface, but the visibility is shit. I can't see a thing. Another wave breaks over the top of me, churning up the water. Bubbles and white froth surround me and the force of it tries to shove me down to the bottom. I stretch my arms out, searching, struggling to find her. She can't have gone far; she's tethered to her board. The leash tied to my own ankle pulls me up short, so I reach for my leg and unfasten it.

I'm running out of air, but I can't find her. My chest burns with the need to breathe and the edges of my vision start going dark. I'm going to suck in a lungful of water if I don't get back to the surface fast.

The water churns again and something rolls a few feet away from me. I surge in that direction and reach out, connecting with something. I grab on. It's Becca's arm. I yank her toward me, but I barely know which way is up anymore. Bubbles rise around me and I have just enough oxygen left in my brain to realize I can follow them. I wrap my arms around Becca and kick as hard as I can, desperately trying to get us above the water.

My head breaks the surface and I suck in a deep breath. I cough and gasp, but make sure to get Becca's face out of the water so she can breathe.

"Oh fuck, Becca."

Her leash is still attached to her ankle, so I rip it off. I don't give a fuck about our surfboards right now. I swim us in toward the beach, keeping Becca on her back. I can't tell if she's breathing.

We make it to the shallows where I can stand, and I scoop her up in my arms like a child. Her back clenches and she coughs up water.

"Holy shit, Becca. Breathe, baby. Breathe."

I get her to the beach and lie her down on the sand. She keeps coughing, but I can hear air getting through. After what seems like an eternity, she starts to breathe normally and her eyes open.

I grab her and pull her against me. She takes a few more breaths and I can't let her go. The terror I pushed aside in order to get her out of the water surges through me, turning my blood to ice.

"Oh my god, Becca."

"Lucas?"

"I'm so sorry," I say, still cradling her in my arms.

Her body shakes and for a second, I'm afraid she's choking. I pull back and look at her face, expecting to see her gasping for air.

She's laughing.

There is absolutely nothing funny about any of this. But she's motherfucking *laughing*.

"What the hell?" I ask. "Why are you laughing?"

"I don't know." She turns her face and coughs a few

more times. "It's just so insane. I was scared, but then everything was great. I caught that wave. Did I really catch the wave?"

"Yeah, you did."

"I did it. I was scared, but I did it." She touches the side of her head and winces. "But did your surfboard hit me in the head?"

I want to die right here. I promised I'd keep her safe and I almost fucking killed her.

"God, Becca, I'm so sorry." I gently touch her temple. I can feel a lump already forming. "You rolled off your board and I couldn't find you. I thought I killed you."

She meets my eyes and smiles. "I'm okay."

"No, you were under the water and you couldn't breathe and—"

She touches her fingers to my lips. "You don't understand. I know something bad happened—the thing I was afraid of, even. But I'm okay."

I hug her against me again, holding her close. I don't want to stop. If anything had happened to her...

Although the sun is shining down on us, the breeze is cold. Becca starts to shiver, so I reluctantly let go.

"Do you think you can stand?"

She nods, her eyes sparkling. I can't believe she's so calm. I'm filled with the desire to scoop her up in my arms and kiss her.

But I hold back. There's a hell of a lot of emotion sparking between us right now, and I'm not sure how to handle it. I'm afraid something as intimate as a kiss—at least, a kiss when we aren't in the midst of fucking each other into oblivion—would be a mistake.

I help her get into dry clothes and put her in the car with the heat blasting. I change out of my wetsuit and we head back down the highway. I left the surfboards in the water. I'll have to replace them, but at this point, it's not worth it to me to get them. I want to take her to the ER to make sure she's okay, but she adamantly refuses, claiming she feels fine. In the end, I convince her to go to the urgent care clinic in town, just to be sure.

The doctor assures me she's not seriously injured. There's no water in her lungs, and she doesn't have a concussion. Hearing it from a doctor eases some of my fear and I feel the knots of tension in my back finally release.

The sun is setting as we drive back to our building. Becca is quiet, looking out the window, a small smile on her face. Nothing about today went as planned—she literally could have died—but she tells me over and over again how great it was.

It's hard to imagine that this is the same girl who looked so lost and upset at locking her keys in her car. She's come a long way. I can't really take credit. Sure, I've had the ideas, and I've provided the push she needed. But she's been in the driver's seat the whole time. I wouldn't have been able to force her to do anything she didn't want to do.

The truth is, she didn't need to become Sandy at the end of *Grease*. She just needed to be herself, free of all the perceptions other people had of her.

She was perfect already.

## 18

## BECCA

It's pretty busy in Finn's pub. I come in and spot Juliet, sitting with our other best friend, Madison. I squeal and run over to them. Madison stands and gives me a big hug.

"There she is," Madison says.

"Sorry I'm late," I say.

"You're fine," Juliet says. "We just got here."

I take a seat at the table and hang my purse on the back of my chair. It's so good to see Madison. "How was the drive down?"

"Not bad," Madison says. "I feel like I haven't seen you two in ages. I can't believe you both had to go and move three hours away from me. You're straight up bitches, you know that, right?"

"We just need to get you out here too," I say. "Then everything will be perfect."

Madison smiles. "Not likely, But at least you moved somewhere that's cool to visit."

A waiter comes out and takes our orders. The three of us catch up on what's been going on in our lives. Madison and her husband Eric just found a new apartment. Juliet fills us in on her wedding plans—she and Finn are going to have a low-key wedding on the beach next summer. I tell them about my job, and what it's been like living by myself. I sidestep around the subject of Lucas, because I'm not really sure what to say.

What is there to say about him? I don't think my girlfriends will understand our relationship. We're good friends, and yeah, we've been sleeping together. A lot, as a matter of fact. It was kind of like a dam breaking—once we started, we couldn't stop. One of us shows up at the other's back door almost every night, and whether we have different intentions or not, we always wind up in bed. Or on the couch. Or the kitchen counter. Or Lucas's desk.

Lucas's desk was really fun.

At first I was worried it would make things awkward between us. But it hasn't. Hardly anything has changed, other than he gives me an endless stream of orgasms. Seriously, I had no idea a woman could actually climax every time. Sometimes more than once. To say he's changed my outlook on sex would be a vast understatement.

The front door opens, letting in a draft of cold air. I glance over my shoulder and my heart skips. It's Lucas.

He notices me right away and grins. I give him a little wave, and he walks over to our table.

"Hi, ladies." He moves behind me to the empty seat and tugs on my hair as he passes.

"Do you remember our friend, Madison?" I ask.

She reaches across the table and they shake hands.

"I think we sang a song together," Lucas says as he sits down.

"Right," Madison says. "Oh man, that night was fun."

Everyone starts talking about our first trip to Jetty Beach, when we came for Juliet's birthday, and she ended up meeting Finn.

I don't know why I'm so tense, but having Lucas sit next to me like this is doing all sorts of funny things to my insides. He's talking to the others, but his eyes dart to me a few times. I wonder if this feels strange to him too. The air between us seems thick, a barrier keeping us apart. I resist the urge to move my leg so it brushes up against his.

*Cool it, Becca. You're just friends, and this is how friends behave.*

After a while, he stands. "I'll let you ladies get back to your night." He winks at me. "See you later, Becca."

Lucas goes over to sit at the bar and starts talking with Finn and Gabe. I smooth down my hair and hope that my face isn't flushed.

Madison raises her eyebrows at me and leans forward, speaking quietly. "You're fucking him."

"What? I am not."

"You so are," she says. "You and Lucas are totally getting it on. Were you going to tell us?"

I glance at Juliet out of the corner of my eye. She's staring at me, open-mouthed. Oh, god, I can't even look at her.

"I..."

"Becca," Madison says, her tone stern.

"Fine." *You know what? I'll own this.* "Yes, I've been sleeping with Lucas."

"Becca, what are you thinking?" Juliet says, her voice a low hiss.

"I'm thinking I'm a grown woman and I can sleep with a man if I want to." I cover my mouth. I can't believe I just said that. "I'm sorry. I didn't mean to snap at you."

Madison points at me. "Don't apologize. That was

awesome. You *are* a grown woman, and you *can* sleep with a man if you want to."

"Of course she can, but she shouldn't be sleeping with Lucas," Juliet says.

"Look, I know what I'm doing," I say. "And I know what you're going to say: Lucas doesn't do relationships. I'm well aware of that. I'm not his girlfriend. He's not my boyfriend. We're just... friends with benefits."

"I love this," Madison says with a smile.

"If you knew Lucas, you wouldn't be so excited," Juliet says.

"Why?" Madison asks. "Is he an asshole or something? He seems really nice."

"No, it's not that," Juliet says. "He's just so anti-commitment. Like Becca said, he doesn't do relationships."

"Yes, and the point is, I know that," I say. "I have no illusions about what's going on between us."

"How did this even happen?" Juliet asks.

I take a deep breath. "I wanted to loosen up a little and take some risks, maybe try things I've never done before. So I asked him to help. At first, it wasn't sexual at all. We did some other stuff, like that night he got me to sing with him. But then we both realized this was an aspect we weren't exploring. And if I want to be a little naughty, what better way than sleeping with Lucas?"

Madison and Juliet both gape at me.

God, I'm so tired of them looking at me like their innocent little friend. "He also got me high."

Madison bursts out laughing and Juliet keeps staring at me.

"What?" I ask. "It's legal."

"Please tell me he didn't get you high and that's why you started sleeping together," Juliet says.

"Oh my god, no," I say. "That was before. And it was just the one time."

"But the sleeping together is a regular thing?" Juliet asks.

"Yeah, pretty much," I say. "Honestly, Jules, I know what this is. We're friends. We have sex sometimes. That's it. It will run its course. I'll be ready to date again for real someday, and we'll go back to being friends who don't have sex. It's no big deal."

"I totally approve of this plan," Madison says.

"How were you the first one of us to get married?" Juliet asks Madison. "That's a serious question."

Madison shrugs her shoulders. "I know, it surprises me too. I always figured it would be Becca. But who cares about me. Becca, is he well hung?"

Juliet rolls her eyes. "I don't think I want to know that about Lucas."

Madison leans closer. "Then close your ears. Tell me."

I know I'm blushing, but I don't even care. I hold up my hands to demonstrate. "He's like this."

Juliet covers her face and Madison's mouth drops open.

"He's hung like a fucking whale," Madison says.

I laugh. I never talked to them about Brandon like this—or any of my old boyfriends. Was I really such a prude?

"And he knows how to use it, too," I say. "You guys, he's done things to me I didn't even know existed."

"Please tell me you got him to put that tongue between your legs," Madison says.

"Yes," I say. "That was the first thing he did."

"And?"

I lean my head back and look up at the ceiling. "It was so fucking good."

They both squeal. "Becca!"

"What? You guys say that word all the time. Why can't I?"

"Who are you, and what have you done with my sweet Becca?" Juliet asks.

I shrug. "I'm learning how to be the real me. I've always done what everyone else expects. And moving here showed me I could do something else. I could start making my own decisions. Lucas has helped me figure out how to do that. He's amazing. He's been sweet and caring, and yeah, he tries to push me sometimes. But I need that. This has been good for me. *He's* good for me."

Juliet presses her lips together. She looks concerned. "I'm glad you're feeling good about all this, but what you just said is what I'm worried about. I'm afraid you'll get hurt."

"You know what, Jules? I might. But I've spent my whole life shying away from things that could hurt me. I've always had people looking out for me, trying to make sure nothing bad happens. But bad things happen anyway, even if you're trying to avoid them. I still had my heart broken, and puked all over Brandon in the middle of a nice restaurant."

"True," Juliet says.

"I'm tired of hiding," I say. "I don't want to keep going through life doing only what's expected, always letting other people shield me from the world. This thing with Lucas might be a big mistake, but I want to find that out for myself. I want to stop being *timid Becca*. With Lucas, I don't feel like a spineless little girl anymore."

Madison beams at me and Juliet's smile brightens.

"I'm sorry, Becca," Juliet says. "I don't mean to be critical. I just want you to be happy."

"I *am* happy," I say. "I'm happy with where my life is right now. I've never really felt that way before."

"I love this," Madison says. "Good for you."

"And you guys, seriously." I glance at Lucas, sitting at the bar. "Whatever else happens, the sex is so good."

"It better be, if he's got a dick like that," Madison says.

The three of us laugh and Lucas glances at me over his shoulder. I wonder if he can tell we've been talking about him.

Our food comes out and our conversation turns to other topics. It's great to be with my two best friends again, but I'm so distracted. My eyes drift over to Lucas constantly. He's sitting at the bar next to Gabe, talking with Finn. The muscles in his back pull against his shirt when he shifts on his stool. He runs a hand through his hair, and all I can think about is what it feels like to have my hands in his hair, when he's—

I turn my attention back to Madison and Juliet, trying to force myself to quit thinking about him. But there's an ache between my legs, and being near him like this is maddening. I notice him glance in my direction a few times. Is he thinking about me, too?

When I look again, he's gone. My phone dings with a text and I peek at the screen. It's from him.

*Get your ass to the bathroom.*

I do everything I can to keep from smiling, but I'm ready to burst. A hit of adrenaline rushes through my veins. Oh my god, he wants to—

"I'll be right back, I just need to go to the restroom."

"Sure," Juliet says. "Do you want me to order you another drink?"

"Yeah, sounds great."

I clutch my purse with nervous fingers and try to keep my face still while I head to the back. My heart beats wildly and the butterflies in my stomach are fluttering like crazy.

I tap on the men's room door a few times. Lucas peeks out, then grabs my wrist and yanks me inside. He shuts the door and locks it, then pushes me up against it, his mouth crashing against mine.

I drop my purse and he grabs me, lifting me against the door. I wrap my legs around his waist. Our mouths lock together, our tongues lashing in a frenzy. I've never wanted anyone like this before. My body is on fire for him, like I can't live another second without him inside me.

"Fuck, Becca," he says. He puts me down long enough to pull out his cock and I'm so grateful I wore a skirt tonight. "You were driving me nuts out there."

"I know, me too."

He smiles and kisses me again before getting out a condom.

"Are you sure we should do this here?" I ask.

"Positive." He lifts me up again and pulls my panties to the side. Any objection I might have had flees as he slides his cock inside me.

My eyes roll back. "Oh, god, Lucas."

He thrusts into me, pushing me back against the door. "That's it, baby. Tell me what you want. I want to hear it."

"Fuck me."

Lucas groans into my neck. "Say it again."

"Fuck me, Lucas. Fuck me hard."

His fingers dig into my thighs and he drives his cock in and out. I've never had sex in a public place before. I'm half terrified someone's going to knock on the door, or my friends will notice I've been gone too long and look for me in the women's room.

But Lucas's thick cock pounding into me erases all my worries. I'm consumed with the feel of him. His breath on my neck. His low growls in my ear. His muscles flexing and tensing with every thrust. Tension builds fast as he slides in and out. My pussy heats up and clenches around him.

"That's it, darling," he says, his voice low in my ear. "Come for me, baby."

He reaches between us and rubs my clit a few times. That's all it takes. I lean my head back and he covers my mouth to keep me quiet. He doesn't stop thrusting, and the friction draws out my orgasm. I feel him start to come, his body stiffening. He groans, and he drives into me, hard.

When we both finish, I put my arms around his shoulders and collapse against him. He keeps me pressed against the wall, my legs still wrapped around his waist. His chest rises and falls against me, and he buries his face in my neck.

He helps get my feet to the ground and deals with the condom, then pulls up his pants. I adjust my panties and make sure my clothes are straight.

He turns back to me and puts one hand on my waist, the other up against the door. His mouth comes to mine, and he kisses me, slow and soft.

It's the first time he's kissed me like this after we had sex. We kiss all the time during, but when it's over, we usually just get up and go back to whatever we were doing before. We don't linger together or cuddle. Even when I've craved more contact with him—when lying in each other's arms would have felt good—I don't ask. It feels like that would be crossing the line we set. Lucas made himself perfectly clear when this started. We're not a couple.

But when he kisses me like this, that line gets awfully blurry.

He pulls away and touches my face with a gentle hand. "That was fantastic."

I'm still breathing a little too fast and I'm sure my face is flushed. "Yeah, it was."

"You naughty girl," he says with a smirk. "Fucking in a bathroom."

"Oh, I see. This was another end-of-*Grease* Sandy thing."

He stares at me for a few seconds, his eyes intense. "Not really. I just couldn't stop thinking about you. I wanted you."

He kisses me again and steps back.

My head is swimming and the way he's looking at me is giving me whirlpool feelings in my tummy. "I should get back to my table. I've been gone too long."

He laughs. "Yeah, we're a little obvious. You go first. I'll wait a few seconds."

I pick up my purse and put the strap over my shoulder. Lucas grins at me again—his lazy post-sex smile. I fix my hair and hope what I just did isn't obvious when I go back to my table.

Then again, maybe I don't care if they know.

## 19

## BECCA

After a tiring day at work—my preschoolers are great, but they sure can wear me out—I sit at my dining table with a cup of coffee. Today was a field trip to the beach, and taking twenty four-year-olds anywhere is an exercise in patience. Once we got out there, it was great. They ran around and dug in the sand and had a fun time. The biggest challenge was rounding them up again when it was time to go back to school so their parents could pick them up.

Definitely an afternoon coffee sort of day.

My phone rings and I look at the screen. It's my dad. Again.

I posted pictures of me and Lucas when we went surfing, and apparently that was a mistake. My dad has been trying to call me ever since, and judging by his voicemails, he isn't happy. I know I can't avoid him forever, so I answer.

"Hi, Dad."

"There you are, Becca. I've been worried sick."

"Dad, I texted you like five times to tell you I'm fine," I say. "I've just been busy."

"Princess, I'm very concerned that this move has been bad for you," he says. "I really think you need to reconsider coming home."

I breathe out a long breath and slump in my chair. "Dad, it has not been bad for me. Quite the opposite, actually."

"Becca, surfing is dangerous," he says. "You could have been hurt."

I made Lucas promise not to tell anyone about me being hit in the head by his surfboard, so it wouldn't get back to my parents. But of course, my dad still worries. "Yes, I know that. I was with my friend Lucas, and he's very experienced. I was safe the whole time."

My dad clears his throat and I wonder if he's more upset by the fact that I was surfing, or that I was out there with a guy he doesn't know. "Listen, princess, I just want you to be happy. And safe. I worry about you when you're so far away."

It is so hard to talk to my dad when he gets like this—especially because I know why he's doing it. I wish I could just say it—tell him that it isn't his fault that Alicia died. And that he can't be right next to me every moment of my life. He can't protect me all the time, and he shouldn't. But I'm afraid he'd be devastated if I said it, and I just can't do that to him.

"Dad, I know you worry, and I know it's because you love me," I say. "I love you too. But you have to understand, I'm happy here. I'm happier than I've ever been in my life. I needed this. You really don't have to worry so much. I'm fine. I promise."

He takes a deep breath. "Well, just remember your mom and I are here if you need help with anything."

"Yes, Dad, I know. I actually don't need your help right

now. Maybe that's hard to understand, but I'm doing really well on my own."

He's quiet for a long moment. "I'm proud of you, princess."

Tears sting my eyes and a lump rises in my throat. I don't think he's ever said that to me before. "Thanks, Daddy."

"Love you."

"I love you, too."

I end the call and it takes me a few minutes to collect myself. I wipe the tears from my eyes and put my empty coffee cup in the sink.

There's a soft tap at my back door and I see Lucas standing on the other side of the glass. He rakes a hand through his hair, and he's absent his usual smile.

I open the door and he steps inside.

"Hey," I say. "Are you okay?"

"I don't know."

He sinks down onto the couch and pinches the bridge of his nose.

I sit down next to him. "Did something happen?"

"I've just had one hell of a day." He looks at me, his brow furrowed. "I'm sorry, I shouldn't bug you with this."

He starts to get up, but I grab his wrist. "No, it's okay, you can tell me. What's going on?"

He pauses for a long moment. "Work this week has been a disaster. I made some bad calls."

"Did you lose a lot of money?"

He shrugs. "Some. I'll recover."

Something tells me there's more going on than stress from his job. He has his ups and downs, but I've never seen him visibly upset about work before.

I'm not sure what to do. I want to reach out and touch

him—comfort him somehow. What's the *friend* thing to do, here?

I put my hand on his arm and squeeze it.

"I also got in an argument with my dad," he says, his voice quiet.

"Over what?"

"Money," he says. "His store is really struggling. I guess it has been all year. The accountant he hired screwed up, and now he owes a bunch of back taxes. He's afraid he's going to lose the store."

"Oh, no."

"I have the money to bail him out," Lucas says. "I can make sure the store doesn't go under, but he won't take it. When I told him I have it, he started questioning my morals. He basically accused me of doing something illegal. He couldn't accept that I actually earned what I have."

"Lucas, that's awful."

"Yeah, it sucks." He rests his elbows on his knees and runs his hands through his hair. "This isn't your problem. I don't know why I came over here."

I've never seen him like this before. My heart aches for him. "You came over because this is what friends are for."

He turns and meets my eyes, his brow furrowing. Leaning over, he rests his head in my lap, then puts his legs up on the couch. His arm drapes across my legs and he holds me tight.

I run my fingers through his hair and his body relaxes. It feels good to hold him like this—to know I can make him feel better. I hate that he's upset, and I can't imagine what it must have felt like to hear that from his dad. My relationship with my parents has been complicated since I moved to Jetty Beach, but this is different. From what Lucas has told me, I know he's struggled to gain his father's acceptance. It must have hurt terribly to have his offer of help rejected like that.

He lays with me in silence for a long time. I slide my fingers through his thick hair. As happy as I am that he came to me, sitting with him like this is stirring up a whole mess of feelings I shouldn't be having. I want to tell him how amazing he is. How proud he should be of everything he's accomplished. I want to tell him how much he means to me. How much I care about him.

But the more I sit here and caress his hair, thinking of all the things I'd love to say, the more the ache in my chest grows. I love having Lucas in my life. I can't imagine it any other way. But I wonder how much longer things can go on like they are. He seems perfectly content with our relationship as it is. Why wouldn't he be? We're great friends, we spend tons of time together, and we always have fun. The sex is off the charts. And he doesn't have to worry about anything else. No expectations, no commitments. We move from one adventure to the next, and enjoy each other's bodies in between. It's the perfect setup for him.

It was for me too, at least at first.

I'm not supposed to want more. I'm not supposed to wish we were more than friends. That's when things get complicated, and we both agreed not to let that happen.

But the truth won't leave me alone, no matter how hard I try to deny it. As I sit with him, comforting him when he's hurt, rubbing his back and sliding my fingers through his hair, the truth gets so loud I can't pretend I don't hear. My throat feels like it's closing up and I bite the inside of my lip as hard as I can to keep from crying.

I can't deny it anymore. I'm in love with Lucas.

## 20

## BECCA

My Saturday plans with Juliet are canceled—she got a surprise visit from her mother, poor thing—and I tell myself a dozen times that I won't text Lucas. Going a day or two without seeing him might do me some good. But my resolve lasts all of an hour.

"Hey," he says with a smile when I let him in the back door. "I was wondering if you were busy today."

"I was supposed to hang out with Juliet, but her mom showed up in town unannounced."

"Is that a good thing or a bad thing?" he asks.

"A bit of both," I say.

"Sounds like my mother," he says. "So, what do you want to do today?"

I know exactly what I want to do. That isn't why I texted him, but being near him makes my body come alive. My heart flutters, my skin tingles, and my pussy is instantly throbbing.

I really wish he didn't do this to me. It would make navigating all these emotions so much easier.

But since he does—

I launch myself at him, throwing my arms around his neck. He kisses me back, his hands grabbing my ass.

He leans down and hoists me up over his shoulder.

"What are you doing?" I say with a laugh.

"Taking what I want."

He carries me upstairs to my bedroom and practically tosses me onto the bed. He yanks off my clothes, using his teeth to pull off my panties. I giggle and squirm while he wrestles me onto my belly. He slides his tongue up the length of my spine, making me shudder.

"You taste so good." He moves my hair out of the way and kisses the back of my neck. "I want to lick every inch of you."

He teases me for a while, kissing and licking my skin, until I'm so hot for him I'm ready to beg. I hear the crinkle of the condom wrapper, but before I can roll over, he climbs onto me while I'm still tummy down. He slips his cock in from behind, and it slides in easily.

This angle is amazing. I push against the headboard and arch my back to take him in deeper. He fists one hand through my hair and the feeling of being in his control is such a turn on. I surrender to him, letting him move my body the way he wants. He yanks on my hair harder, almost enough to hurt, and I let loose, calling out with his thrusts.

"Don't... stop... oh my god... yes."

He feels so good, I can't control myself. I'm pinned down, helpless, totally at his mercy. His cock is so thick and he's driving it so deep, giving me everything I need. A thousand points of light explode as the first orgasm rolls through me. My core clenches and tightens, sending waves of pleasure through my whole body. Lucas shifts his hips and just as my orgasm starts to recede, I'm hit with another one. He comes with me, his cock thrusting hard, pulsing, throbbing, his breath hot against my neck.

When it's finally over, he moves off me. But instead of getting up, he rolls onto his back and drapes an arm over his forehead.

I'm aching with the desire to snuggle up against him. To feel his arms around me as we catch our breath. But I don't know how he'd react if I try to cuddle with him. I'd know if it made him feel awkward, and I think that kind of rejection would be worse than the pangs of emotion I'm feeling now.

I force myself to get up and put my clothes back on. Lucas doesn't say anything, so I go downstairs, trying to act like everything is just as it should be. We had great sex, as always, and now that it's over, we're back to being friends.

Nothing else going on here. Just the usual.

I take a seat at the dining table and thumb through a small stack of mail. Lucas comes downstairs, pulling his shirt over his head. He smiles at me and heads for the kitchen.

"Want anything?" He opens my fridge.

"No, I'm good."

He grabs a beer and opens it, then pulls out the chair across from me and sits.

I get to a cream-colored envelope with handwriting I recognize. The return address is my parents'.

"Oh, no." I already know what it is, but I open it anyway.

"What's wrong?" Lucas asks.

I pull out the invitation. "It's my parents' thirtieth wedding anniversary. They're throwing a big party. Obviously I have to go."

"I take it you don't want to go?" he asks.

I run my fingers along the gold leaf lettering. "Well, I'm

happy for them, and this is a big deal. So in that sense, of course I want to celebrate with them."

"But?"

"Brandon's parents will be there."

Lucas stares at me for a moment, his beer halfway to his mouth. "*The* Brandon?"

"Yep."

"Why would they be at your parents' anniversary party?"

I put the invitation down. "My parents are friends with them. They're all country club people, so they see each other a lot. If my parents didn't invite them, it would be a pretty big insult. But honestly, I don't think it would occur to my parents not to ask them to come."

"That's shitty," Lucas says. "They'd invite your ex's family to their party?"

It's odd, but hearing him say *your ex's family* doesn't hurt. When I first moved to Jetty Beach, any mention of Brandon brought tears to my eyes. Now, I don't feel much of anything. Maybe this is what it's like to get over someone.

Maybe it's because I love Lucas a thousand times more than I ever loved Brandon.

I push that thought out of my head, but my cheeks warm and I know I'm flushed. "Yeah, it's awkward, but there isn't anything I can do about it. They'll be there. And there's no way I can miss it."

I desperately want to ask Lucas if he'll come with me. I chew on my lip, wondering if I should. I imagine walking into my parents' house with Lucas by my side. I could face this party with Lucas. It might be the *only* way I could face it.

Lucas and I both start talking at the same time.

"Would you come with me?"

"Do you want me to come with you?"

He gives me a wide smile and we start laughing.

"Great minds," he says. "So, I guess that's a *yes*?"

"Would you?" I ask. "I know that's a lot to ask."

"Of course I will," he says. "Just remind me so I don't forget."

"It's a dress-up sort of event," I say. "You'd need to wear a suit."

He winks. "Darling, I have you covered. I'll be there, suited up for battle."

I reach across the table and touch his hand. "Thank you. Really, this means a lot to me. I feel like I can do this if you're there."

"With or without me, I know you can do it," he says. "But I'm happy to be there for you."

I get up and head for the fridge to cover the sudden rush of tears that flood my eyes. Why does he have to be so wonderful? Why couldn't he be a jerk? I guess we wouldn't be such good friends if he were awful. But he's too good to me. I can't keep my feelings under control when he's being amazing like this.

I'm not in the mood for a beer, so I get a glass of water. "Well, thanks. I should call my mom and let her know I'm bringing someone. She hates it when people don't RSVP on time."

"No problem." He gets up and leaves out the back, winking at me again as he slides the door closed.

I get my phone and take a deep breath while I bring up my mom's number. This is going to be interesting.

"Hi Becca," she says when she answers. "How are you, sweetheart?"

"I'm fine. How are you?"

"I'm well. Busy. This anniversary party is turning out to be quite the undertaking."

"I bet. Did you invite a lot of people?"

"Oh, I suppose," she says. "It's all the usual people. You know most of them."

*All the usual people.* It's so frustrating that they still socialize with Brandon's family. It's not that I'm upset about Brandon anymore. I've moved past my heartbreak; in fact, I'm glad he broke up with me. I kind of wish he'd have done it sooner. In a lot of ways, my life didn't begin until that night I threw up all over him. But there's no way it won't be awkward to see them at this party.

However, I have Lucas.

"That's great, Mom," I say. "I bet it's going to be lovely."

"I hope so," she says. "I'm very happy with the caterer we chose, and I think your father wants a Mediterranean theme for the food."

"That sounds good," I say. "Listen, I called to officially RSVP."

"You didn't have to do that," she says. "Of course you're coming."

"I know. But I also wanted to let you know I'm bringing someone."

"Sure, honey, that's fine," she says. "Who are you bringing? Juliet?"

"No, I'm bringing Lucas."

"Lucas, that man in the surfing pictures?" she asks, and I can hear the skepticism in her voice.

"Yes, Mom, Lucas the man in the surfing pictures," I say.

"Well, honey, are you sure?"

A sliver of anger twists in my belly. Why does she have to question everything I do? "Yes, I'm sure. Lucas is my boyfriend, Mom."

I cover my mouth and close my eyes. Fuck—Lucas is right, sometimes no other word will do—I shouldn't have said that. I'm so glad I'm having this conversation over the phone, because there's no way I could have said that to her face. I just lied to my mother.

Worse, I lied about Lucas. And I'm going to have to tell him.

"Oh, I didn't realize," she says. "How long has this been going on? Were you planning to tell us?"

"It's new, Mom. That's why I haven't said anything yet." *Or I'm lying through my teeth and Lucas is going to kill me.*

"All right," she says. "In that case, please bring him along. I'm anxious to meet him."

"Yeah, it will be great," I say. "Well, I should let you go. I know how busy you are. But I'll see you at the party, okay?"

"Sure, sweetheart," she says. "I'll let your father know to expect you both. Talk to you later, honey."

"Bye, Mom."

I put the phone down and lower my head to the countertop. What did I just do? I didn't need to tell my mother that Lucas is anything other than a friend. She probably would have been happier hearing that. I know she and my dad are still holding on to the idea that Brandon and I will get back together. It doesn't seem to matter that he moved across the country to be with another woman. They seem to think we'll both come around, and wedding bells won't be far behind.

Plus, there's no way Lucas isn't going to be mad at me over this.

## 21

# LUCAS

We pull up to Becca's parents' house after a quiet drive from Jetty Beach. There's a gate out front that's open to allow guests in, and a long driveway leads to the house. Other cars were parked along the street behind us, but she directs me to an area where there's more parking. The house itself is massive, with huge double front doors flanked by pillars.

As requested, I'm wearing a dark gray suit and tie. I don't have a reason to dress up like this very often, but I actually enjoy it. I got my hair cut yesterday so I'd be nicely groomed for this party. It seemed like Becca would appreciate that. She did tell me I looked great when I came to her door to pick her up.

Becca turns toward me and she has a little groove between her eyebrows. She only looks like this when something is really bothering her. Without thinking about it, I take her hand.

"Are you really that nervous?" I ask.

"Kind of?" She takes a deep breath. "Lucas, I have to tell

you something, and I'm afraid you're going to be mad at me."

I get a twitch of nerves at that. I'm suddenly worried this has something to do with her ex. Did she find out he's going to be here too? "Okay, well, just tell me."

"I called my mom after you said you'd come with me, to let her know I was bringing someone." She takes another deep breath. "I told them you're my boyfriend. I'm sorry, it just kind of came out."

Hearing her say the word *boyfriend* opens something inside my chest. I quickly tamp the feeling down before it overtakes me.

"I'm not mad," I say. "So you want me to act like we're dating tonight?"

"Yeah," she says. "I guess that's what I'm saying."

I twine my fingers with hers, bring her hand up to my lips, and kiss it. "I have you covered, darling. Tonight, you have the best fucking boyfriend on the planet."

She smiles, but it's not the bright smile I'm used to. It's subdued. I feel bad that she's so jittery about this party. I know she's nervous about seeing her ex's family. Me? I can't wait. I want to show her off in front of them so they can see the sexy, confident woman their son was stupid enough to leave behind. *That's* going to make her feel better.

She glances down at her hand, still clasped in mine, and pulls it away. "Okay, I guess we should go in."

"Wait." I reach over and slide my hand across her cheek and through her hair, bringing her face close. I slant my mouth over hers and kiss her softly.

I never kiss Becca like this. We've had our mouths all over each other, but it's always in the midst of sex. This is different. This is sweet, like her. Tender. It's not a prelude to something else. I'm not about to suggest we bang in the car before we go inside. I just like the way her lips feel against mine. She feels good.

She feels right.

Hearing her call me her boyfriend kind of did too, but I'm putting that out of my head. Things with Becca are fine the way they are. And we have a dinner party to get through tonight.

"What was that for?" she asks when I pull away.

"Courage."

I go around and open her car door for her. She looks fucking incredible in a knee length black dress and silver heels. Her blond hair is pulled up, and she has a silver necklace with a diamond at her throat. There's a little shimmer in her makeup and her glossy lips taste like mint.

Her eyes dart to the front door and back to me.

I take her hand and lift it, kissing it again. "Are you okay?"

"I think so," she says. "I don't know why I'm so nervous."

"Because your ex's family is here and it's going to be weird to see them," I say.

"Am I so transparent?"

"How else would you feel tonight? It's totally normal to be nervous. But trust me on this: By the end of the night, you're going to be walking out of here with your head held high."

She laughs. We head for the door, hand in hand. She's like this tiny little bird, so fragile, but as soon as the wind catches her wings, she can soar. This is literally the cheesiest thought I've ever had, but I need to be her wind tonight.

I squeeze her hand when we get to the front door. "Is there anything else I should know before we do this? Any warnings about your parents?"

Her shoulders slump a little. "My parents are nice

people, but they treat me like I'm eleven. My dad calls me princess a lot. They wanted me to marry Brandon so he could take care of me. He's the golden boy in their eyes. Honestly, I don't think they believed me when I told them *he* broke up with *me*. I think they assume it's my fault, and I ruined this big chance I had."

"Holy shit." Instinctively, I bring her closer. "So you showing up with another man is going to be..."

"Nail in the coffin," she says. "I'm sorry, Lucas, I have to be honest. Deep down, I think I told them you were my boyfriend because I want to kill any notions they have of me getting back together with Brandon. Maybe that was a crappy thing to do."

"Not at all." I slide my hands around her waist and turn her so she's facing me. "Like I said, I'm in. And I'm glad I can do this for you."

"Really?" she asks. "I was so sure you'd be weirded out."

"Nope," I say. "This is going to be fun."

"Our next adventure?"

"Exactly."

We turn toward the door, and this time *she* grabs *my* hand. I push the door open, and we walk inside.

Her parents' house is kind of ridiculous. It looks even bigger on the inside. The foyer has a shiny marble floor leading to a huge staircase. Off to one side, there's a living room with a big fireplace, also marble. Above it is a painted portrait of what must be Becca with her parents. She looks about ten. On the other side is a dining room with a large table, all decorated in cream and gold. Everything is light and pristine and so clean. But there's very little color. It's mostly beige.

She leads me past the stairs toward the back side of the house, where it opens to a large kitchen and a family room with a big TV. There are appetizers on a bar height table, and more pictures of Becca at varying ages on the walls. There's another fireplace, and what looks like Becca's senior picture in a gold frame above it. She was right—I don't see any pictures of her sister.

Guests mill around the appetizers and there's a caterer working in the kitchen. The rest of the guests seem to be outside; I can see a crowd of people through a set of French doors.

Becca's grip on my hand tightens as we walk through the house. I lift her hand and kiss it again, hoping to give her some reassurance.

A man who can only be Becca's father comes in from outside. He's about my height, with short blond hair peppered with gray, and a trim build. He's dressed in a dark suit, and he holds his hands out to the sides, the corners of his eyes crinkling.

"Princess," he says with a smile.

I note that he's not looking at me.

"Hi, Daddy," Becca says. She drops my hand and walks forward to hug her father. "Dad, this is Lucas Murphy. Lucas, Stephen Foster."

I step in and hold out my hand. "It's a pleasure to meet you, Mr. Foster."

"Lucas." He takes my hand in a firm shake. So far, so good. "Thank you for joining us."

He's polite, but there's a hint of displeasure in his eyes.

A petite woman in a cream-colored dress covered in sequins comes in. Becca favors her father, but I can see the resemblance. This must be her mom.

"Sweetheart," she says, coming in to hug Becca. "You finally made it."

"Well, Mom, it's a long drive," Becca says.

"This is why you should have taken that apartment we found," she says. "You'd have been right up the road. We could have picked you up."

Becca's face colors. "That's okay, I made it just fine. Mom, this is Lucas Murphy. Lucas, my mother, Karen Foster."

I hold out my hand and she takes it with a light grip. "Nice to meet you, Mrs. Foster. Congratulations on your anniversary."

"Thank you," she says with a smile. Her eyes dart between me and Becca a few times. "Well, please, mingle. Enjoy yourselves."

Becca's dad squeezes her shoulder before he walks away with his wife.

She lets out a long breath. "Okay, we got that part over with."

"Your parents are nice," I say.

"Yeah, they're always polite," she says.

"Then what were you worried about?"

She shrugs. "I don't know. We should go do a lap outside."

I put my hand on the small of her back as we head out the double doors. The backyard stretches out in front of us, a huge expanse of precisely manicured landscaping, with a big, multi-level deck and lots of seating. The guests are all well dressed—the men in suits, the women in dresses—and they stand in small groups of threes and fours, clutching drinks and talking.

I lean in and speak softly into Becca's ear. "Do you see them?"

"Over there." She gestures with her head to the left. "Older man in a gray suit, and his wife is in the navy pantsuit with the platinum blond hair."

"Do you have to talk to them, or can you keep your distance?" I ask.

She takes a deep breath. "I don't have to, but I want to. I want to show them I'm okay."

I smile at her and caress her back. I love seeing that fire in her eyes. "That's my girl."

Her brow furrows a little, but she smiles back. "I could use a drink first, though."

We make our way to the bar on the other side of the deck. She asks for a glass of white wine. I opt for a whiskey, neat. We stand off to the side and a few people come over to say hello to Becca. She's friendly, but I can feel the undercurrent of tension running through her. I keep a hand on her at all times—on her back, or her arm. Partially, I want to make sure I'm touching her when Brandon's parents turn around and notice us. But I also want her to feel my presence—to know I've got her back tonight.

She sucks in a quick breath and her whole body stiffens. "Oh my god."

"What's wrong?"

"Brandon's here."

A jolt of adrenaline zings through me and I follow the direction of her gaze to the French doors. A guy dressed in a dark suit comes through and his parents walk over to greet him. His blond hair is swept back in an ultra-douchey pompadour and he reminds me of all the pretentious lawyers I had to socialize with when I lived with Valerie in New York. I hate him instantly.

"What is he doing here?" she asks, her voice small.

I know it's a rhetorical question, but I answer anyway. "Maybe he came with his parents."

"He moved away. He's not supposed to be here," she says,

the heat in her tone growing. "If my parents invited him here to see me again..."

Brandon turns, his eyes landing on Becca, and his face changes. His smile fades and he swallows hard.

Even if Becca didn't ask me to play the part of her boyfriend tonight, as soon as Brandon looks at her, I know I would have done it anyway. Fuck that guy. Brandon's parents watch her as if they're waiting to see if the timid little girl will fall apart.

They're all in for a big fucking surprise.

I put my hand on the back of her neck and rub my thumb up and down the top of her spine. I don't need to smother her to claim my territory. I simply lean in and kiss her neck, right below her ear. She plays it perfectly, turning her face up so she can look at me, her lips parting in a smile. I meet her gaze, smiling back, and I get so lost in her eyes I actually forget what we're doing for a second.

"Hi, Becca."

"Brandon," she says.

I keep my hand on Becca's neck and watch her. I don't look at Brandon at all, so I don't know if he's looking at me. I gaze at her, like she's the only person in this place that matters. Like I'm thinking about slowly slipping that dress off her shoulders, letting it pool on the ground at her feet. Kissing the pale skin of her shoulders and watching her cheeks flush.

"Lucas?" Becca says.

I snap back to reality. I got a little carried away, there. I shake Brandon's hand. "Nice to meet you. Brandon, is it?"

"Yeah." His hand tightens on mine before he lets it drop. "So, Becca, it's nice to see you. How have you been?"

"I've been wonderful, actually," she says without hesitating.

"Have you?" he asks.

The amount of concern in his voice raises my hackles. What does he think? That she can't possibly get along without him?

"Absolutely," she says. "I moved to a new place and I really love it. Things are good."

"Who are you living with now?" he asks. "I thought you'd still be living here with your parents."

"No, of course not," she says. "I moved out to Jetty Beach, actually."

"With Juliet?" he asks.

She shakes her head. "No, I live alone."

His eyebrows lift. "Wow. I had no idea."

Okay, he's a little too surprised at this bit of news. I need to take this asshole down a notch. "Yeah, it's amazing what can happen when a person has their own space. Freedom to really explore life and all it has to offer, you know?"

"Uh, sure," Brandon says.

"We've done a lot of great exploring together, haven't we, Becca?" I grin at her and sweep a tendril of hair off her shoulder.

Her cheeks flush the slightest shade of pink—god, I love that—and she bites her lower lip. "Yes, we really have. It turns out there's so much to explore."

"It's true," I say. "There's a whole world out there."

Her eyes sparkle. "And it's so much *bigger* than I imagined it could be."

I barely manage to suppress a laugh, and I smile at her like an idiot.

"It's interesting," she continues. "There are so many more ways to enjoy it than I knew about before. So many options. Luckily Lucas really knows what he's doing. He's shown me a lot of things that I wasn't sure I'd like, but... holy shit. I've loved them all."

The color drains from Brandon's face and he gapes at Becca.

I meet Becca's eyes. She smiles at me, triumphant. I'm so fucking proud of her.

"You are, without a doubt, the most amazing woman I've ever met," I say.

As soon as the words leave my mouth, I realize that it's not a bullshit line. I'm not acting, and I haven't been this whole time. She really is, and the way I've been looking at her, touching her, stealing little kisses—I mean it all. I love being like this with her—like we're actually a couple.

Like she's mine.

I'm dazed, like I just got hit upside the head with something hard. Becca *isn't* mine. We're putting on a good show, and maybe that's all this is. Maybe I drank that whiskey a little too fast. But I'm staring at Becca and something is blossoming in my chest. Something huge, and I have no idea what to do about it.

Because I'm scared to death.

She's still talking to Brandon. I clear my throat and try to blink away my confusion.

"I'm surprised you're in town," she says. "I thought you moved to the East Coast."

"I did," Brandon says, and he casts a glance over his shoulder toward the house. "I'm living in New York City now. But we came to town to see my parents."

I don't miss the way he says *we*, and I'm sure Becca notices too. To her credit, she seems fine. I can tell she's got this conversation, so I gently take her empty wine glass and hand it to a passing server. I figure I'll go get us both another drink and let her finish up with her ex. I meet her eyes and tilt my head toward the bar. She nods back.

I get another glass of wine for Becca and opt for ice water for myself—I have to drive us home, and I want to be able to leave whenever she's ready. When I walk back toward her, I notice Brandon is no longer alone. A woman stands next to him and his hand is on the small of her back. She's wearing a fitted black dress and her dark hair is up in a sleek bun. Their backs are to me, and I quickly look past them to check Becca's face. Being surprised by her ex is one thing. Having to face his new girlfriend is another. But her expression is friendly and relaxed. She doesn't seem particularly bothered by this sudden turn of events.

I walk over and hand Becca her wine. From the corner of my eye, I'm struck by the vivid red lipstick Brandon's girlfriend is wearing. I look over to find her staring at me, open-mouthed, her eyes wide. My blood runs cold and the air rushes from my lungs, like I just got punched in the gut.

It's Valerie.

## 22

# LUCAS

*I* stare at the woman standing across from me. There's no mistaking that face. Sharp cheekbones, deep brown eyes, precise makeup. It's been a few years since I've seen her, but she looks exactly the same. What the fuck is she doing here?

The punched-in-the-gut feeling intensifies and it takes all my self-control to maintain calm on the outside.

"Lucas?" Valerie asks. Her cheeks flush and her eyebrows draw together in a severe line.

"Valerie," I manage to get out.

Becca looks back and forth between us, her lips parted in surprise.

"Do you know each other?" Brandon asks.

Valerie takes a deep breath and smooths her features. She puts a hand on Brandon's arm. "I'm sorry, honey. Yes, Lucas and I have a bit of history."

'A bit of history'? *More like you crushed my heart, you cheating bitch.* "What the hell are you doing here?"

"I could ask you the same question," she says.

"It's my girlfriend's parents' anniversary party." I step closer to Becca and clasp her hand in mine. "I was invited."

"We're in town so I can meet Brandon's parents," Valerie says. "It just so happened to coincide with this dinner, and they asked us to come along."

I stare at her, feeling sick to my stomach. How is this even possible? The silence stretches to the point of awkwardness, but I can't make myself look away and my throat is so tight I can't talk. Brandon glances between me and Valerie a few times, his mouth moving like he wants to say something.

Finally, Becca looks at Brandon and breaks the silence. "Well, this is... strange. How did you two meet?"

"Work," Brandon says. "I met Valerie on a business trip when I was still living in Seattle. My firm was working with hers on a merger. We hit it off immediately, and that's when I..." He clears his throat. "That's when I told you. I moved to New York to be with her shortly after. Things moved pretty fast, but when you meet *the one*, there's no reason to hold back."

*The one*, my ass. She's probably fucking around on this guy too.

Brandon looks at Valerie the way a puppy looks at his owner, and I think I might vomit. Valerie smiles back. I know that fucking smile. It's how she used to look at me. God, did I look at her with the same dumbfuck expression Brandon is giving her now?

Valerie reaches up to adjust Brandon's tie. That's when I realize there's a giant rock on her finger.

She seems to notice my eyes on her ring and holds out her hand, as if to show it off. "This is why we came to Seattle. Brandon proposed last week. He wanted to tell his family in person, and I hadn't met them yet, so here we are."

Becca squeezes my hand. "Well, congratulations to both of you."

"Thanks," Brandon says. "It looks like everything worked out for the best."

"It definitely did," Becca says.

There's an exchange of goodbyes and I try not to make eye contact with Valerie. I'm seething inside, my gut churning. I moved across the entire fucking country to get away from her—to get away from what she did to me. And here she is, floating around a dinner party on the arm of some jackass, showing off her giant diamond.

It never occurred to me to wonder what it would be like to see her again. The last time we met, she dropped off the key to our apartment. We didn't say a word to each other. She just glared at me and handed me the key. From the moment she confessed to sleeping with some fucker at work, she'd gone ice cold, as if the entire thing were somehow *my* fault. As if she'd never felt anything for me, and she was impatient to get me out of her life.

Seeing her now, I'm hit with a mix of anger and grief. Back then, I thought I was in love with her. She swept into my life like a fire, consuming me. When she left, I was nothing but a pile of cold ashes. I'm angry that I let her do that to me. Angry that she can still hurt me, even years later. I'm flooded with the same bitter sense of loss.

Somehow, Becca and I make it through dinner, keeping our distance from Brandon and Valerie. Afterward, her parents take her aside and talk to her for a while. She tells them goodbye, explaining that we have a long drive. I hear them offer to bring her home tomorrow if she wants to stay the night. They don't extend the invitation to me, and she refuses.

We head out and Becca is quiet for most of the drive,

watching out the window. I can tell something is bothering her. She's stiff, her knees angled away from me. She chews on her lower lip and doesn't look in my direction.

Despite all the surprises, I would have thought she'd be pleased with herself. If you have to see the ex who broke your heart, tonight was the way to do it. For her, at least. She was stunning and sure of herself, and even got in a few digs about her newly enhanced sexuality. Granted, Valerie was a curve ball neither of us saw coming. But Becca knew Brandon was with someone else. The fact that she's *my* ex-girlfriend shouldn't have made things measurably worse for Becca. She looked them both in the eye, calm and confident. She has every reason to feel proud, yet I can tell she's struggling.

The truth is, I'm struggling too.

I want to reach over and touch her. Kiss her like I did when we arrived at her parents' house. It felt good to be with her tonight. All those moments—kissing her hand, touching her skin, looking into her eyes. Standing by her side. They felt right.

I want to ask her if she's okay, but I don't know if I trust myself. There are words skipping through my mind, like rocks on the water—pinging across the glassy surface of my thoughts in a steady repetition. Words like *mine*, and *future*, and another one that begins with an *L*, that I can't even bear to let myself think.

Maybe I should just say it. Tell her what I'm feeling. Admit that I—

But I'm not supposed to want her like this. I've told myself a million times that she and I are great as friends, but we can't cross into something more. I swore I'd never put myself in that position again.

Seeing Valerie tonight reminded me why.

The thought of Valerie's face makes me sick with anger. I trusted her with a piece of myself and I've regretted it every day since she left me. I upended my life to stay in New York with her—fought with my dad over it, changed all my plans. When it was over, I felt like an idiot for believing that what she and I had was real. It never was, not if she could throw it back in my face the way she did.

When I moved home, the answer seemed so obvious. Don't get involved again. Keep it casual. I could meet a woman and enjoy her for a night or two, and avoid all the potential for heartbreak. I was always honest. I never let any woman believe what we had was more than a short fling. If they were in for that, great. If not, I'd move on.

And it worked. Most of the time, anyway. Sure, there were a few women (Angela Miller comes to mind) who said they were fine with a bit of casual sex, but were really hoping for more. That didn't always end well. But for the most part, I had everything I wanted. Work, friends, hobbies. Afternoons spent surfing. Beers at the pub. Plenty of money.

Then in walked Becca.

"Are we going to say anything about tonight?" Becca asks out of the blue when we drive through the entrance to Jetty Beach.

"I don't know what there is to say."

"Well, we could talk about the fact that my ex-boyfriend is engaged to your ex-girlfriend. I think that's kind of a big deal."

I shake my head. What are the fucking odds? "It was a surprise. I never thought I'd see her again. But Valerie and I were over a long time ago. It's not a big deal."

"You've been acting like it *is* a big deal."

"What are you talking about?"

"You did a total one-eighty. First you were mister perfect sweetheart, kissing me and touching me in front of everyone, even Brandon. I kind of thought..." She looks out the window and takes a deep breath. "And then Valerie showed up and you went all cold. Are you okay?"

*No. I hate that she can still get to me, and I hate that she's making me doubt what I feel for you.* "Yeah, of course I'm okay. Why wouldn't I be?"

Becca sighs again. "There are plenty of reasons why you might not be okay. This was a really weird night for both of us."

"I don't know what else you want me to say. It happened. It was awkward. It caught me off guard, that's all. Can we move on?"

"Don't you think it caught *me* off guard?" she asks. "I had no idea Brandon would be there, let alone show up with a fucking fiancée. And you act like you don't even care."

"You had the perfect moment with him," I say, frustration leaking into my voice. "You looked amazing, and you said all the right things. You even got in a small-dick joke. What more do you want?"

"I don't know. I just don't understand what's going on with you," she says. "You've hardly said a word to me. I don't know if you've even looked at me since you saw her."

What the hell, is she jealous? *Please don't make this more confusing for me, Becca.* "What do you want? Do you want me to assure you I don't care? To tell you I don't have feelings for her anymore? Because I don't know why that would matter to you. It's not like we're together. We're just friends."

Becca turns to look out the window so I can't see her face. I clench my jaw and grip the steering wheel. Fuck. Why did I say that? It's true, isn't it? We are just friends.

Then why did it feel so shitty to say it?

I turn up our driveway and pull into my parking spot. "Becca, listen—"

"No, you're right," she says. "We *are* just friends. It was a mistake to ask you to come with me tonight. I should have gone on my own."

"It wasn't a mistake," I say. "I didn't want you to go alone."

"This whole thing was a mistake." She throws open her door and gets out.

Whoa, what the fuck is happening right now? I get out and follow her as she strides to her door, pulling her keys out of her purse. "What do you mean, this whole thing was a mistake?"

She stops in front of her door but doesn't turn around. "Lucas, I can't do this anymore."

"What are you talking about? Can't do what?"

"All of this," she says, and I can hear her trying not to cry. "You and me. I didn't think it would be too much, but it is."

I know what she means, but I don't want to hear it. I can't hear it. Not right now. Not tonight.

"It's not your fault," she says, her voice suddenly quiet. "I knew. You were honest with me, and I knew what you were like. I thought I could handle it. But I can't. I'm feeling too many things when we're together and it's making me want things I can't have. I hate the idea that we can't be friends anymore, because I kind of don't know what I'm going to do without you." She pauses and wipes beneath her eyes. "And, who knows, maybe someday we can be friends again. But for right now, I can't."

"Can't be friends anymore?" I ask. Panic tightens my chest. "Of course we can. We can back off—take things down a notch."

"Maybe you can, but I can't," she says. "I need a break from you. No more games. No more adventures. No more sex. No more hanging out."

"But Becca—"

"I don't want to have to move again, but that might be what it takes," she says. "For now, I need you to leave me alone. Don't come over, or call, or text. I need some time."

"Wait."

She pauses, her key in the door, but I don't know what to say. I'm sick to my stomach, my head spinning.

"This is what you wanted," she says, finally turning to look at me over her shoulder. "No commitment. You don't owe me anything. But that means I don't owe you anything, either. This was just a game to you, and I can't play anymore."

She opens her door and walks in, then closes it behind her.

I stand there for a long moment, staring. *What just happened* is a stupid thing to ask myself. I know what happened.

I just lost her.

### 23: Becca

TEARS STREAM down my face the second I get the door closed behind me. Somehow I managed to keep from sobbing in front of Lucas, but now my resolve is gone. I drop my purse and step out of my shoes. I don't bother turning on any lights. I simply go upstairs, fall into bed, and bury myself in the comforter.

Tonight was, without a doubt, the worst night of my life. I'd thought the night Brandon broke up with me would forever hold that title. But even puking in a fancy restaurant on the man I once thought I'd marry can't compare to the utter shit show that was my parents' anniversary party.

Lucas played the part of my boyfriend far too convincingly. In a way, I think I would have felt better about it if he'd resisted—if he'd been upset with me for lying. But he just smiled that brain-melting smile of his. And that kiss in the car. Sweet and lovely and wonderful. Why would he kiss me like that? No one was watching. He didn't need to start pretending.

All night, every touch was both amazing and terrible. It was everything I'd ever wanted from him, but never dared to hope for. His looks, his caresses, his stolen kisses. I loved it. Nervous as I was, I basked in the glow of being with him. Of not holding anything back when I looked at him. After all, we had a show to put on. He didn't have to know there was truth in my eyes.

Then, seeing Brandon made my heart feel like it stopped. But by the time I had to speak to him, I was overcome with a sense of calm. Part of it was Lucas's hand on my skin—the warmth of his touch lending me strength. But I knew that even if Lucas hadn't been there, I would have been okay. I wasn't self-assured because I had a fake boyfriend for the night. I was confident because whether I'm single or part of a couple, I'm proud of myself. I'm making my own choices and living my own life. Knowing that erased the last traces of any power Brandon may have once had over me. I'm truly better off without him.

Even meeting his new girlfriend wasn't as awful as I would have imagined. It was interesting to see how completely unlike me she was. Taller, dark hair, sharp and businesslike. Brandon could hardly have found anyone more my opposite. I noticed her ring immediately—long before she mentioned it—and even that didn't hurt.

And then Lucas came back and all hell broke loose.

The woman holding the arm of my ex, wearing a ring I once thought would have been meant for me, was the same woman who broke Lucas's heart.

I'm not dumb. I know why Lucas doesn't want to be in a real relationship. He was hurt, and judging by the way he looked when he saw Valerie, he was hurt more deeply than I ever realized. The depth of pain in his eyes twisted my heart. It made me want to rush him out of there as fast as I could—to hold him and comfort him and do anything to make him feel better.

But it was like a switch had flipped, and the Lucas I know was gone. After we finished our awkward conversation with Brandon and Valerie, he was practically silent, avoiding my gaze like he couldn't bear to look at me.

Was it because he remembered how much he'd loved Valerie? Was I suddenly a reminder of everything he had lost?

Whatever the reason, everything about tonight left me feeling hollow and confused.

I spent the drive home trying to sort through the storm of emotions raging inside me. Shock at seeing Brandon again. Jealousy at the way Lucas looked at Valerie. Sadness at how hurt he was. Agony over how much I wished we weren't pretending to be a couple. I didn't know what to do with it all. I still don't.

If Lucas had given me the slightest hint that he was being genuine—that maybe he feels something for me too—I would have confessed everything. Blurted out that I love him. That he doesn't need her because he has me. He can have all of me if he wants. He only has to ask.

But he didn't. He reminded me in no uncertain terms that we're just friends. That was the deal.

And if a woman like Valerie had his heart—a woman so utterly different from me—how could I think he'd want someone like me now?

The week goes by, and avoiding Lucas is easier than I thought it would be. I keep the curtain on my back door closed. When I need to go places, I hurry to my car so I don't risk running into him out front. I can hear him when he's home, but I keep the TV on a lot to drown out the little sounds that carry through the walls.

Living with the hole in my heart is much harder.

I miss him terribly. I miss the sound of his voice. His smile. The way he'd grin at me through the sliding glass door, sending little pings of nervousness through me whenever he'd come over. I miss the way his skin felt against mine. His lips. His hands. My body aches for him, but more than missing the sex, I miss his friendship. Talking with him until all hours of the night. Sharing funny things I found online. Watching movies and sharing a bowl of kettle corn. We were together all the time, and now I'm suddenly so lonely.

I miss the way he made me feel. Like I wasn't the breakable little girl who couldn't make it on her own. Like I was strong enough to handle anything life threw at me.

But I'm not sure if I'm strong enough for this.

I try to stay busy, but in the quiet moments of the day, I wrestle with what I did. Should I have tried harder? Maybe I should have told him we needed to get rid of the *with benefits* part of our friendship, and go back to what we were before. Could I see him and spend time with him, keeping my feelings in check, if I knew we wouldn't sleep together?

Because it was the sex that made the difference, right? Sleeping with him made me fall for him?

Except I know that's not true. I would have fallen for Lucas even if he'd never had the crazy idea to go down on me that day. If we'd never shared a kiss or a single intimate touch. It's not his body I fell in love with—although there's certainly a lot to love about it. I fell in love with *him*. And with who I am when I'm with him.

I can't come back from that, and it's killing me.

I come home from work on Friday, glad I survived the week. The weather is getting colder, so I go upstairs to find a thicker pair of socks. My feet are freezing. Just as I'm sliding them on, my phone rings. I know who it is before I even look. It's my dad.

"Hi, Dad."

"Hi, princess," he says. "How was your week?"

"It was okay. How about yours?"

"I can't complain," he says. "I haven't talked to you since the party. Did you have a nice time?"

"Yeah, it was great." Biggest lie I've ever told.

"I'm sorry your mom and I didn't spend more time with you," he says.

"It's fine. You had a lot of guests."

"Yes, that's true," he says. "But it was our first time meeting your new boyfriend. We'd still like the chance to get to know him better. That's why I called, actually. We'd like to have dinner with the two of you sometime soon."

I sink down onto the edge of my bed. Why did I ever say Lucas was my boyfriend? What a disaster. "Um, Dad, about Lucas…"

"Is something wrong, princess?"

"Well, that isn't really going to work out," I say.

"What happened?" Dad asks, and I can hear the hint of anger in his voice.

"It was my choice, Dad. He's a very nice guy, but we want different things." At least I'm not lying about *that*.

"Oh, Becca."

I bite my lip to keep from tearing up, but the sympathy in his voice is too much for me. "It's okay, Dad. I promise I'm all right."

"Princess, you're crying."

I sniff and swallow hard. "A little bit, but it's not that big of a deal. Really. I'll be fine."

My dad is quiet for a long moment. Then I hear him talking softly to my mom. His voice is muffled, like he's holding the phone away so I don't hear them.

"Do you want us to come down?" he asks.

"No," I say. "Don't do that. I swear, I'm okay."

"Because we can be there in three hours," he says.

"I know, Dad, but you don't have to do that."

There's more muffled talking. "Doesn't he live right next door?"

"Yes, he does. But it's fine. Dad, listen to me. I'm okay. Yes, I'm sad, but I'll watch a comedy tonight and I'll feel better. And I'll spend some time with Juliet. Girl time, you know?"

"Okay, sweetie. If you're sure. I'll call you tomorrow," he says.

I take a deep breath. "Okay, Dad. I'll talk to you later."

Lucas's front door closes and I squeeze my eyes shut, letting the tears trail down my face. Damn it, why does this have to be so hard? I wonder if I should move and get it over with. Knowing he's right there, on the other side of that paper-thin wall, is almost too much to bear.

I need to get out of my apartment tonight, so I text Juliet.

She's free later, so we make plans to meet up. I resolve to play it cool about my breakup—if that's even what to call it. I'll be honest with her, but I don't want to wind up sobbing on her shoulder.

~

A SHARP BANGING sound startles me awake. I glance at the clock. It's just after nine. I roll over, pulling the comforter up over my shoulder.

Juliet and I drank too much last night. I didn't cry over Lucas—at least not until somewhere in the middle of our *second* bottle of wine. Then it all came spilling out. Juliet hugged me while I cried, and then we drank more. Finn drove me home late, and now I have a pounding headache. I close my eyes and hope I can go back to sleep.

There's another set of bangs, and I realize it's someone knocking on my front door.

With a groan, I force myself out of bed. I throw on a cardigan and a pair of leggings and hurry downstairs to see who could possibly be knocking this early on a Saturday.

I open the door and blink in surprise. My parents are on the step, smiling at me.

"Princess," my dad says.

"What are you two doing here?" I ask.

"Come now, Becca," Mom says. "Is that any way to greet your father?"

I step aside so they can come in. "I'm sorry. You woke me up and I wasn't expecting you."

"You were still sleeping?" Dad says. "I figured you'd have already been out for a run this morning."

"Yeah, well, I drank a lot last night, so I'm kind of hungover."

I'm not sure what possessed me to say that. My parents look at me like an alien must have taken their daughter's place.

"Becca," my mom says, like she's scolding me.

I rub my eyes and go into the kitchen. "Maybe I'll make some coffee. Would either of you like some?"

My parents share a look and my dad walks forward, like they silently agreed that he's going to give the lecture.

"Princess," he says, "your mother and I have thought this over, and we really think it's time you moved closer to home."

"This is home," I say, gesturing around me. "I live here. That makes it home."

"Our home will always be your home," Dad says. "You should be closer to your family."

"I don't live very far away," I say. "It's driving distance. Lots of people live so far they have to take a plane to see their parents."

"Yes, but those people aren't you," he says. "Plus, we've become increasingly alarmed at the direction your life has taken since you moved here."

I pause with my hand halfway in the coffee canister. "I'm sorry, what?"

My mom moves next to my dad. "Well, for starters, there's that man you were dating."

"Lucas?" I ask. "Why are you so worried about him? He was really good to me."

"I'd have thought you would have chosen someone more appropriate for you," she says.

I open my mouth to reply, but my dad cuts in.

"Living out here has no doubt been an interesting experience," he says. "But don't you think it's time you came back where you belong? Surely you've moved on from Brandon by now."

My back tenses up and a flash of anger hits me. "Is that what you think? That I moved away because of Brandon?"

"Well, of course you did, honey," Mom says. "It's not that we blame you for how you felt. That was difficult. But running off certainly didn't help matters."

"This isn't about Brandon," I say. "It was never about him. This is about me. I need to stand on my own two feet and finally be a grown-up. Not just a girl playing house. I moved here because I need space to figure out who I am. You shouldn't be alarmed about my life. You should be happy and proud. I have a job I love. I have a place to live and I can afford the things I need. I have good friends nearby. Isn't that what parents want for their kids?"

"Yes, princess, of course we want that for you," Dad says.

"And as for Lucas, just because his family doesn't belong to your country club, that doesn't mean he's not *appropriate* for me. Honestly, Mom, do you realize how bad that sounds? You don't even know him, and you're assuming he's not good enough?"

"That isn't what I meant," she says.

I take a deep breath. "I know you guys wanted me to be with Brandon. But he wasn't all that great. He strung me along for four years. At least Lucas was always honest with me."

My parents look at each other. I can tell this conversation is not turning out the way they expected.

Dad's phone dings and he pulls it out of his pocket. He turns to my mom. "They're still waiting outside. They've already been here for fifteen minutes. I should go let them in."

"Who's waiting outside?" I ask. "Let who in?"

He hesitates, exchanging another one of *those* looks with my mom. "The movers."

I gape at him, my eyes wide. "What?"

"Becca, calm down," Mom says. "We took care of everything for you. You can stay with us until we find you a new apartment closer to home."

I look between the two of them a few times, at a loss for words. They hired movers? This is crazy, even for them. I brush past and burst out the front door. Sure enough, there's a moving truck parked in front of the building.

My dad tries to say something, but I whirl on them. "This is unbelievable. I am not a child. I'm a grown woman, and you can't show up here with a moving truck and pack up my life."

"Princess—"

"No, Dad," I say, holding up a hand. "This is not okay. I'm sorry that you worry about me. But you have to let me go. I'm not a little girl anymore. I'm happy here. Yes, I'm upset about what happened with Lucas; that part isn't so great. But I like it here, and I'm not moving. I miss seeing you guys all the time, and I'll try to come visit more often, but I'm not moving back. I'm really living for the first time, and I love it."

My parents stare at me for a long moment. I stand my ground, looking them in the eyes with my chin lifted. I can't let them keep trying to run my life. If they move me home now, I'll never be free again.

"I'm sorry, Becca," my dad says. "Your mom and I thought this was the right thing for you."

"I know you did," I say. "But it's not. You have to trust me to make decisions for myself."

I take a deep breath and go outside to talk to the movers. I apologize and try to explain that there was a misunderstanding. They look a little confused, but after speaking with my dad—they're probably charging him for their time, but honestly, I can't even feel bad about that—the moving truck pulls back out onto the street and leaves.

Back inside, my dad opens his arms and I step in to hug him.

"I'm proud of you, princess," he says.

My mom rubs my back and smiles. "If you're sure this is what you want."

"I'm sure, Mom. Listen, you guys came all the way down here. Why don't we go out to breakfast and then I can show you around town."

They agree and I go upstairs to shower and change. I'm still stunned they actually hired movers, but I can't stay angry at them. I never could. I hope this was the breakthrough we needed, and they can finally accept I'm an adult who can take care of herself. Time will tell, I suppose.

The sound of Lucas's shower carries through the wall. Because *of course* he's showering at the same time as me. I turn on the water and try to force thoughts of him out of my mind. I need to focus on being *put-together Becca* today. It wasn't that I was lying to my parents—I *am* happy living here. But I don't want them to see how hurt I am over Lucas. It will only make them worry, and there's nothing they can do about it anyway.

It's simply something I have to learn to live with.

## 23

## LUCAS

*I* wait outside my dad's store, leaning against my car in the empty parking lot. It doesn't open for another hour, but I know he'll be here soon. He's always in early. Anxiousness thrums through me. I haven't spoken more than a few words to him since we had our discussion about money. That went worse than I thought it would. Although I was always afraid of hurting his pride if I told him how much money I have, I never expected him to accuse me of being a fucking criminal. But he couldn't accept that I've earned everything I have.

I went over to Becca's place that afternoon, almost without thinking. I sat with her and told her what happened, and damn it if she didn't make me feel a million times better. Remembering it now is like a knife twisting in my gut. It felt so good to sit with her—my head in her lap, her fingers running through my hair.

With a heavy sigh, I try to put thoughts of Becca out of my mind. I'm here to see if I can clear the air with my dad. Ignoring him has been the easy way out, but I'm worried he'll do something stupid, like close the store. Somehow, I'll convince him to take the money. Even if he doesn't want to speak to me again afterward.

This week has been the worst. Things fell apart so fast after the anniversary party, my head is still spinning. The shock of seeing Valerie wore off pretty quickly. It wasn't hard to see her because I still have feelings for her. It was hard because it reminded me of how badly she hurt me—how vulnerable I was. And of all the reasons I had for staying out of another relationship.

It's Becca that has me tied up in knots.

When I'm home, I hear every little sound coming through the wall—a constant stream of tiny reminders that she's next door. And that I can't go see her.

I've tried to respect her wishes and leave her alone. I don't call or text. I avoid going to my car when I think she'll be out front, and I don't go anywhere near her back door. As much as I wish I could, I don't try to change her mind.

I fucking hate it.

Dad pulls up in his old pickup truck. He gets out and nods to me. "Son."

I follow him inside. He doesn't say anything, so I don't either. He takes off his coat and tosses it onto the chair in his office, then goes into the back. Without a word, I start helping him pull out boxes and restock shelves. He's never been a big talker, but I keep hoping he'll say something. There's such a huge gulf between us, and I'm not sure how to bridge it.

We finish up, and it seems like Dad isn't going to say anything else. I guess that means it's up to me.

"Dad, about the store…"

"We've been over this," he says. "I don't think we need to discuss it any further."

"Can we just move past the fact that you don't trust me

for a second? I need to make sure you aren't going to do something crazy."

"Crazy like what?" he asks.

"Like close down."

He looks away.

"No, Dad. I'm not dropping this."

He takes a deep breath. "I'll be open through the end of the month, but after that I have to close. I can't afford to keep the doors open."

I pinch the bridge of my nose, frustration eating at me. "Damn it. You *don't* have to close. I told you before, I can help you."

"I won't take your goddamn money," he says, his voice sharp.

It takes every ounce of my self-control not to tell him to fuck off, and leave. "Do you actually believe I'm a criminal? What do you think I did for that money? Do you think I was out on the street selling drugs, or are you picturing some kind of white collar crime?"

He grunts and looks away again.

"If that's what you think of me, you don't know me very well," I say.

"Who has that kind of cash sitting around?" he asks.

"I do. I work hard for the money I earn. Maybe it's not selling tools, but there's nothing unethical about it. It's risky, not criminal. There's a difference. I understand this stuff, Dad. It comes naturally to me and it always has."

He doesn't answer, and the knot of anger sits in the pit of my stomach, eating away at me.

"You know what? Forget it," I say. "You don't respect me enough to talk about this and you obviously don't trust me. I don't know what I'm doing here."

I walk away and I'm almost out the door before he speaks.

"Lucas."

I stop, but keep my back turned to him and let the silence hang between us.

"Maybe I have a hard time because you do something I don't understand," he says.

He pauses and I turn to look at him, but wait. I'm tired of having to draw every word out of him. If he has something to say to me, he needs to say it.

"You're right. I should trust you," he says. "I raised you to be a good man."

That's got to be one of the deepest, most heartfelt things my dad has ever said to me. It's right up there with the only time he said he was proud of me, when I graduated college.

"Thank you," I say.

"You can really part with that kind of money?" he asks.

"Yeah, I can. Dad, I have it five times over, and I'd give it to you in a heartbeat."

He blows out a breath and looks down at the floor. "It will be a loan."

"All right." *Whatever makes this work for you, Dad. Just fucking agree to take it.*

He walks over to me and looks me in the eye, holding out his hand. I take it and he shakes mine in a firm grip.

"Thank you, son," he says.

A lump rises in my throat and I swallow hard, choking back the sudden rush of emotion. Dad nods and drops my hand.

"I talked to your mother again," he says.

"Uh-oh," I say. I'm not thrilled that my mom keeps calling him to dig for information about me, but I understand his need to change the subject. "I just talked to her the other day. Why is she calling you again?"

"It's that social media stuff," he says. "She saw pictures of you with a girl. She said you told her you aren't dating anyone, so she wanted to know if I knew what was going on."

Ah, fuck. "Yeah, that was Becca. She's... she's a friend of mine."

"A friend?" Dad asks. "Is that all?"

"Yeah, that's all."

Dad raises one eyebrow at me, but doesn't press the issue. This is one time I'm grateful for his emotional repression.

"All right, son, I'll let you get back to your day."

"Thanks, Dad."

I head back to my car and get in. At least I cleared the air with Dad. That was weighing on me more than I realized. Now that he and I are good—and I know he'll let me help him out—I can quit worrying about him.

I consider not going home. It's still early, and I don't have anything going on today. But I don't want to sit at home, listening to Becca through the wall.

Maybe I need to get out of town for a little while. Put some distance between us. I could just head out to the highway and drive—see where I end up. That actually sounds pretty good, but I should run home first and grab some clothes.

My plan seems like a great idea, until I turn onto my street and see a fucking moving truck outside Becca's apartment.

Oh, fuck. My chest constricts and my back stiffens. She can't be moving. There's a beige Lexus parked next to her car. It must be her parents. If they're here...

Oh my god, she *is* moving.

I'm feeling panicky, my lungs tight like I can't get enough air. I pull into my parking spot and glance over at the truck. A couple of guys are sitting in the cab; the driver is on his phone. There's a part of me—the crazy part, obviously— that wants to walk up to the truck and tell them there's been a mistake. They aren't needed today. Pay them for their time, and get them out of here before someone starts hauling Becca's stuff out of her apartment. And then...

What? Tell Becca she can't move? That would go over well.

I go inside, but I'm restless. The property manager hasn't called to say she gave her notice, but it's the weekend. Maybe it was a last-minute decision. Voices drift through the wall from Becca's side. I can't hear what's being said, and I'm not such a dick that I try to eavesdrop. I assume they're over there packing.

I hate feeling so fucking helpless. She asked me to leave her alone, and I have. I kept hoping she just needed time— that any day now, she'd knock on my back door and want to at least talk. But she's leaving.

And I honestly don't know if I'll ever see her again.

Pacing around my apartment isn't getting me anywhere, but my idea to go out of town has already lost its appeal. I don't know what I'm going to do. Getting drunk tonight at Finn's pub is about the only thing that sounds halfway decent, and even I realize how pathetic that is.

I head upstairs to take a shower. A few seconds after I turn on the water, I hear Becca's shower through the wall. Because *of course* she's taking a shower at the same time as me. It's impossible not to imagine her: Water streaming down her body, her skin flushed pink from the heat.

Thinking like that is not helping. But I'm not even

tempted to get myself off. I just stand there, letting the water pour over me, wondering if anything will fill the hole in my chest.

## 25: Lucas

I TAKE a seat at the bar and nod to Finn. There are quite a few people in here tonight—most of the tables are full. Finn is busy pouring drinks, so I glance at my phone while I wait.

I look up just as Becca and Juliet come from the direction of the restrooms.

*Oh, shit.*

What is she doing here? I figured she would have left with her parents by now. She must be spending one last night hanging out with Juliet before she leaves town.

Becca's eyes meet mine and she looks away quickly. She heads straight for the front door. "Sorry, Jules, I have to go."

"No," I say as she passes me. "Don't. I'll go."

She doesn't look back, just shakes her head.

"Becca, I didn't know you were here. You don't have to leave. I will."

And she's out the door.

Amazingly, Juliet doesn't glare at me. She looks at me with something that might be pity. I think that's worse.

"I'm going to go with Becca," she says to Finn.

He leans over the bar and kisses her before she follows Becca out the front door.

"You look like shit," Finn says once Juliet is gone. "I'll be right back."

He pours a few more drinks, then comes back and slides a glass across the bar to me. His shitty day special. I haven't needed one of these for a while. I nod to him and take a sip.

"So, you want to talk about it?" he asks.

"There's not much to talk about," I say. "I didn't think things would get complicated with her, but I guess that's me being an idiot."

"What was actually going on with you guys?" he asks.

"I don't know," I say with a shrug.

"You don't know?" he asks. "No wonder she broke up with you."

"She didn't break up with me," I say. "Because we weren't together."

"First off, friends can break up too," Finn says. "And second, yes you were."

"We weren't," I say, pointing a finger at him. "She and I agreed to that."

"I don't give a shit what you agreed to," he says. "You weren't *just friends*."

I know he's right. I'm not *that* stupid. "Fine, we weren't just friends. But I don't understand how this got so out of control."

"That's kind of obvious, isn't it?"

"Apparently it isn't," I say. "But, by all means, enlighten me."

"You fell for her," Finn says.

Before I can answer, Finn has to go take care of another customer. I stare at my drink. I did fall for her, didn't I?

Shit.

Finn comes back and leans against the bar, wiping his hands on a towel. "What was with the *just friends* thing, anyway? Why not just date her?"

"Do I actually have to answer that?"

"Is this really all about your ex?" Finn asks. I don't answer and he seems to take that as leave to keep talking. "Look, I get it. You got hurt. So when you moved back here, you figured you wouldn't put yourself in a position to be hurt again. That's why all the out-of-town girls. No relationships, no ties, no complications. No chance of getting hurt. Right?"

"Yeah, I guess."

"And you thought you could have the same thing with Becca."

"I knew Becca was different, but I thought we could handle it. She didn't need a boyfriend, she needed a guy friend to do cool stuff with. And yeah, to fuck her brains out sometimes. What was so bad about that arrangement?"

"What *was* so bad about it?" Finn asks, punting the question back to me.

"Nothing."

"Don't be a dumbass," Finn says. "You had to have known it couldn't last. What did you think was going to happen when she met someone else?"

My lungs constrict. "Wait, did she meet someone else?"

"I don't know, but the fact that you're about to panic over it should tell you something," he says. "What I mean is, if you weren't willing to commit to her beyond being friends, what did you expect to happen? Is she supposed to just keep being single and sleeping with you on the side? Come on, man, even *I* see how that was going to turn out. Especially because your feelings got involved. And hers did too."

"I don't know. She said it was just a game and she can't play anymore."

Finn leans against the bar. "I know you were trying to keep from getting hurt. That's fair. But at some point, you had to have realized you have feelings for Becca. Why didn't you just tell her?"

*Because if I admitted I had feelings for her, she'd have the power to hurt me.* "I didn't want to get involved with a girl again. Not like that."

"But you did anyway," he says. "Regardless of what you called it."

I take another sip of my drink. "I don't know what I expected."

"Well, at this point you need to ask yourself what you want," he says.

"Beyond getting shitfaced and making you take me home later?"

"Yes, beyond that," he says. "Although I can help with that too."

Finn leaves again and I down the rest of the drink. What *do* I want? If Becca came back in here and said we could go back to what we were before, would that be enough? Would I want to be her friend, spend time with her, and leave it at that?

Because Finn is right—what happens when she meets someone who wants more?

Becca isn't going to stay single for the rest of her life. She's a family girl. She wants the whole package—the ring, the pretty wedding, the picket fence. Probably babies. I've seen her with kids. It would be stupid for her not to have her own. I know that would make her happy.

She's going to meet that guy—the one who will give her everything she wants. She deserves that guy. That life. She deserves to be happy.

I stare at my empty glass, marveling at how fucking awful I feel. I thought I'd hit rock bottom after Valerie left me. At the time, I didn't think anything could be worse. I was devastated. I thought my life was over.

This is worse.

There's an ache in my chest that won't go away. Becca gutted me when she told me she couldn't see me anymore.

The worst part is, I know it's my fault.

Finn's right, I absolutely fell for her. I was so afraid of letting it happen again—so afraid of being hurt—that I kept that line drawn between us. We crossed that line over and over, but I insisted it was there. Yeah, we crossed it sexually, but I don't think it was the sex that broke us.

At least, that isn't what broke me.

*She* broke me. She got in, under my skin, into the core of who I am. Into that place I've kept locked up tight since my last breakup. She did it softly, nestling her way in with her smiles, her laughs, with that sweet pink flush of her cheeks. With the way she's so fun to be around. The way she bites her lip when she's nervous. The way she can be so brave when she feels supported.

All I was trying to do was keep from getting hurt again. And the very thing I did to protect myself is exactly what's killing me now.

I let my head drop to the bar and rest it on my arm. Fuck, I'm the world's biggest idiot.

"Want another?" Finn asks.

I glance up at him. "What do you think?"

"If you get trashed, you have to wait here for me to get off work before I can take you home."

"Good," I say. "I don't want to go home."

Finn leaves and comes back a few minutes later with another drink. He passes it across the bar and scrutinizes me for a long moment.

"What?" I ask.

"I don't know if you want to hear this."

I take a swig of the drink. "Lay it on me, brother. At this point, I have nowhere to go but up."

"I just think sometimes you have to let love ruin you," he says. "It's going to fuck you up, but you have to let it."

I raise my glass. "Well, ruin me it has."

"So you admit it?"

"Admit what?"

Finn leans against the bar. "That you love Becca."

I did just admit that, didn't I? Fuck. "You tricked me into it."

He laughs. "You do love her. You love the shit out of her, and you have for a long time now. You realize the solution is simple, right?"

"If I realized that, would I be sitting here in your stupid pub, drinking?"

"Maybe," he says with a shrug. "Just because you know what to do doesn't mean you're ready to do it. But honestly, man, this is not complicated."

"Once again, enlighten me."

"Tell her."

I take another drink without looking at Finn.

"Come on," Finn says. "I bet that's all she wants from you. She just wants you to love her. You already do. So why the drama?"

"Multiple reasons," I say. "But mostly, I don't know if I can do that again."

"Lucas, I'm going to level with you," he says. "If you don't think she's worth the risk, then let her go. It isn't fair to her to string her along anymore, so staying away from her is the right thing to do. Let her move on. And I hate to tell you this, but that probably means your friendship is over. It's not like either of you can hit the rewind button and pretend the rest didn't happen. She needs to be able to go forward and find someone who's right for her."

I scowl at the bar, unable to look Finn in the eyes. What

he just described feels like hell. It's the worst thing I can imagine right now. No Becca in my life. Ever. She'd be gone, and eventually with someone else. I fucking hate that so much I almost want to punch Finn in the face for saying it.

"But," Finn says, and stops for a dramatic pause that makes me think the face-punch might be warranted no matter what. "Maybe you can't imagine that life. Maybe the very idea of it is pissing you off so much you want to hit me right now."

I look up.

"See?" he says. "I think you know she's worth the risk. You're just afraid to admit it because it means you might get hurt again. But come on, man. It's Becca."

I stare at my drink. "It doesn't matter at this point anyway. She moved out today."

"She did what?" he asks.

"You heard me," I say. "She moved. I saw the truck this morning, and I think her parents were there too. I figure they came down to move her back up to their place."

"Dude, I don't think she moved."

I look up at him. "What?"

"I don't know why there would have been a moving truck, but if Becca was moving away, Juliet would have been flipping out. And I had lunch with all of them before Becca's parents left, and no one said anything about moving."

"Holy shit."

"Hold that thought," Finn says. He has to go wait on customers again, so he leaves me alone, brooding over my drink.

She's not leaving? The surge of hope that pours through me is enough to freak me out a little. Hope for what? That I can keep torturing myself by listening to her through the wall?

Or do I have hope that this can have a different ending?

I hate living without her. It doesn't matter that I planned to avoid falling in love with someone. I went and did it anyway.

If only I'd been honest with myself—and her—I could have avoided this bullshit. God, I should have told her the night of her parents' party. It doesn't matter how messed up it was to see Valerie. I should never have let that woman get under my skin. What happened between us was a long time ago, and I'm an idiot if I keep letting the past rule my future.

And let's be honest: There's some poetic justice in knowing the cheating bitch who broke my heart is with the douchecanoe who broke Becca's.

I push the rest of my drink away. I'm not getting drunk tonight. I don't know if I still have a chance with Becca, but I won't spend the rest of my life wondering. If she doesn't want me, it will hurt. But losing her forever would be worse.

## 24

## BECCA

*I* glance at the clock, wondering what time it is. It feels too early for me to be awake. Sure enough, it's not even five-thirty in the morning. Why did I wake up? I have the vague notion that I heard a noise. I lie in silence for a long moment, but I don't hear anything. It must have been a dream.

Just as I roll over to go back to sleep, I do hear something. I'm sure of it this time.

My heart skips and a jolt of adrenaline races through my veins. Is this me being scared of nothing, like usual? Or is there actually something—or someone—downstairs?

I'm wide awake now, and I won't be able to go back to sleep. I strain, trying to listen. I don't hear anything, but that isn't helping to slow my pounding heart.

What I should do is check. I should walk downstairs and look around. I'll see that nothing is wrong, and I'll be able to relax and go back to sleep for a couple more hours.

But what if someone is down there?

I glance at my phone. I could call Lucas. Even though I

haven't seen him in a while—other than running into him at the pub last night—I'm sure he'd come over and check for me if I asked. I gave him an extra key a long time ago, and I didn't ask for it back. I could lock myself in the bathroom and wait while he does a once over of the whole apartment. Then I wouldn't have to do it. He might even be awake. Working on East Coast time means he's always up early.

I blow out a long breath. No, I have to handle this. I'm going to get up, walk downstairs, see that my apartment is empty, and go back to bed. I don't need anyone coming to my rescue. Especially Lucas.

Just in case, I grab the baseball bat my dad gave me out of the closet. Yes, it has a pink handle. I swear, everything my dad buys me is pink. But it's big and heavy, and if there is someone there, I'll be ready for them.

I swallow hard and hold up the bat while I tip-toe down the stairs. My heart beats faster. A sound comes from the kitchen, and I stop dead in my tracks. Oh my god, I think there *is* someone down there.

My palms are sweaty and my limbs feel jittery. I can't believe this is actually happening. I force myself to take the last few steps down. There's a clink against the counter top and I bite the inside of my lip to keep from screaming. A shadow moves in the dim light coming from the front window.

*Oh my god. Holy shit. Oh, no.*

I hear another sound—a footstep. I raise the bat and take the last few steps to the kitchen.

The dark form of a person is next to the counter. I raise the bat and swing it as hard as I can, aiming for his head.

"What the fuck?"

The person ducks, and I miss. I bring the bat around for another shot.

"Becca!"

I recognize his voice, so I pause, blinking at him. "Lucas?"

"Holy shit, is that a bat? You almost hit me."

My hands twist on the handle. "Lucas, what the fuck are you doing in my apartment?"

"Could you maybe put the bat down first?"

"No."

"Okay." He takes a step backward. His eyes dart to my chest and I can feel my nipples poking out against my thin tank top. Damn it, now my face is probably turning red.

"This was obviously a stupid idea," he says.

"What idea? What are you talking about?"

"I got you something, and I wanted to surprise you," he says, talking fast. "So I thought I'd put it here for you to find when you got up. That's where my plan kind of falls apart, obviously, because basically now I'm just a creeper who broke into your apartment."

"I'm so confused."

He takes a deep breath. "Of course I would screw this up. Fuck. I'm really bad at this romantic stuff, Becca. I'm sorry."

"Romantic? Lucas, I have no idea what you're talking about."

He holds up his hand, like he's afraid I might still hit him, and flips on the light. "I got you some kettle corn, because it's your favorite."

"You broke into my apartment to give me kettle corn?"

"No." He grabs something off the counter and holds it up. It's a ceramic pitcher, filled with kettle corn, and there's a little note sticking out the top. "I got you a pitcher."

"A pitcher? I don't—"

"Just, read the note," he says.

I put the bat down and pluck the note from the pile of

popcorn. It's a plain index card, and on one side, in Lucas's handwriting, are the words, *As You Wish*.

My mouth drops open. "A pitcher? Is this…? In *The Princess Bride*, Buttercup asks Westley to fetch her a pitcher."

Lucas smiles. "Yeah, exactly. I knew you'd get the reference. It was when she realized that Westley wasn't just saying a*s you wish*."

"He was saying—"

Lucas reaches out and touches my mouth with a finger. "No, don't say it yet."

"What?"

He puts the pitcher on the counter, then steps closer and brushes my hair back from my face. His fingers make my skin ping with electricity.

"I don't want you to say it yet because I don't want you to ever doubt what I'm going to say to you," he says. "I need to tell you first."

"Tell me what?"

"That I love you."

I gasp and step backward. "Are you playing some kind of joke on me?"

"No, it's not a joke," he says. "I wanted to tell you that I love you. I thought if I gave you something meaningful, it might make you more willing to talk to me. I guess in hindsight, sneaking in here when you're asleep wasn't the best idea. I just imagined you finding it in the morning, and you'd come to my back door, all confused and adorable. And then I could tell you."

I gape at him. Lucas is standing in my kitchen, and he just told me… what, now?

"Are you serious?"

"Yes, I'm totally serious. And also starting to panic a

little, because I didn't think you'd stare at me like this when I said it."

I swallow hard. My throat feels tight and my heart won't slow down. "Did you just say you love me?"

"Yes, I did." He moves closer. "Do you think I could kiss you now? Because at this point, I feel like if I keep talking I'm just going to continue to freak you out."

I'm too shocked to say anything coherent, but I manage a small nod. He caresses the side of my face with the backs of his fingers and leans in close.

His lips press against mine and my eyes flutter closed. He slips his hand around my waist to my back and pulls me against him. His mouth moves slowly, his kiss soft and gentle.

I'm trembling, dissolving into a million tiny sparks that fly through the air. I've wanted Lucas to kiss me like this for so long. His tongue parts my lips and slides against mine while I drape my arms around his shoulders. He tilts his head so he can kiss me deeper, his arms holding me close, the heat of his body filling me.

Eventually, we pull apart. He leans his forehead against mine and puts a hand on the side of my face.

"I'm sorry," he says quietly.

"For what?"

"For not telling you sooner," he says. "For keeping this from you. And for letting you believe I was pretending. That night at your parents' house, it was easy to act like I was in love with you, because I am. I was afraid of it. That's all."

"I thought I was the fraidy-cat," I say with a soft laugh.

"No, you're so much braver than you think you are. I've been the one letting fear get the better of me. But I shouldn't have been afraid of this." He pauses, his brow furrowing.

"Unless I completely misjudged this and you're about to tell me to get the hell out and go home."

"That's definitely not what I want to say."

"Then what do you want to say?" he asks.

I swallow hard and meet his eyes. "That I am *so* in love with you."

He wraps me in his arms, picking me up off the ground. His breath is warm against my neck. "Oh, thank God. I was worried for a second."

We stand in my kitchen for a long moment, just holding each other. His arms around me feel so good and tears sting my eyes. I'm almost afraid to believe this is really happening.

His lips press against my neck and desire blossoms inside me. I tilt my head and he kisses me again, harder. His hands move down and he grabs my ass through my thin shorts.

He moves back and I'm ready for him to rip my clothes off right here in the kitchen. But he pauses, his expression intense.

"I'm not going to fuck you right now," he says, touching my face.

"What?" I ask, almost breathless.

"I'm going to take you upstairs and make love to you."

He grabs my hand and leads me to my bedroom. I stand next to the bed while he gently takes off my tank top and shorts. His hands whisper across my skin and he gazes at me, his eyes drinking me in like he's never seen me before.

Like this is our first time.

He takes off his clothes and lays me down. He's so careful. So tender. He climbs on top of me, kissing my neck, across my jaw, to my lips. His tongue caresses mine and he shifts his weight, his cock almost pushing inside me. His skin against mine is sublime.

"You're so perfect," he says between kisses. "I love every inch of you."

I draw my fingers through his hair and move my hips, anxious to have him inside me.

"Darling, you feel so good, but I need a condom first," he says.

"If you know you're safe, you can..."

He raises his eyebrows. "Are you sure?"

"Yes," I say. "I'm on the pill."

"I'm safe." He pushes his cock in, slowly. My eyes roll back as he stretches me open. He's careful, but there's so much of him, it always hurts a little at first. I sigh out a long breath and relax, the feel of our bodies together overwhelming my senses.

Lucas starts to move, his cock sliding easily through my wetness.

"No one has ever made me feel the way you do," he says. "You're amazing."

Heat spreads through my core, and the friction of his cock makes my heart race. He pulls up one of my legs so he can thrust deeper. I clutch onto his back, my hands sliding over his flexing muscle. He drives in and out, pushing deep inside me, his rhythm gentle yet electrifying.

If he sped up, I know I could come in an instant. The pressure builds and I feel the edge of my climax, hovering just out of reach. But we ride the line together, drowning in intensity. He touches me, kisses me, caresses me. I'm swept away by his body, his hands, his mouth. I've probably slept with Lucas a hundred times, but not like this. Never like this.

He's right. He's not fucking me. He's making love to me, and every bit of me feels the difference.

"Lucas," I say, his name a sigh from my lips.

"I love you, Becca," he says, his voice low in my ear. "God, I love you so much."

He moves faster, plunging into me harder. I moan with every thrust. No one has ever made me feel this way—so alive. So wanted. So complete.

"You're so hot and wet, I can't hold back," he says.

"Don't," I say, almost breathless. "Come inside me, Lucas. Come in me."

He drives his hips, grinding against me. I start to come and I feel his cock pulse. It's bliss. His body stiffens and he groans into my neck. I hold him tight while my orgasm washes over me, riding the high with him as he comes inside me.

It takes my breath away.

Lucas lifts up just enough to kiss me. He brushes the hair back from my face and kisses my lips, my cheeks, my forehead.

He rolls off me, but instead of getting up out of bed, he pulls me close. I rest my head on his shoulder and he wraps his arms around me. I squeeze my eyes shut against the sting of tears.

"Lucas?"

"Yeah?"

"Can I really keep you?" I ask.

He laughs and draws me in closer. "You're stuck with me now, darling."

"Good."

I relax against him, my heart so full. This is everything I wanted. Lucas, holding me. Loving me. Our bodies close, and our hearts closer. No more lines in the sand. No more boundaries between us.

It's perfect.

# EPILOGUE
## BECCA

The waves roll under me, lifting my surfboard. Sunlight glints off the water and Lucas glances back at me. He's a few feet ahead, paddling out toward the heavier surf.

"You good?" he calls back over his shoulder.

"Yeah, perfect."

I dip my hands into the cold water and pull myself forward. I glide across the surface and another wave picks me up. The ocean stretches out all around me, and the roar of the waves fills my ears. It's the first day that's been warm enough for surfing in a while. I didn't even hesitate when Lucas suggested we go out.

Am I scared? Yep. I'm terrified. But I'm pretty sure I won't get smacked in the head by a surfboard again (what are the odds, really?), and I know if anything else goes wrong, Lucas is right there.

He always has my back.

Another wave comes at me and I make sure to keep my board pointed toward it so it doesn't flip me over.

"I think we're good here." He comes up alongside me and we both turn around, pointing our boards at the beach. "Do you remember what to do?"

"Yep, I got it." I splash some water toward him. "No clobbering me in the head this time."

He shakes his head and smiles. "Ready?"

I nod and feel the surf start to build. I paddle as hard as I can, trying to keep up with the wave, but it rolls under me. Lucas catches it and pops up to his feet, but swerves around and jumps back into the water.

I let the next wave roll by as he paddles back toward me.

"You could have kept going," I say when he gets close.

"No way, darling," he says. "I'm sticking with you."

We get set for another try and the wave comes. I paddle hard and feel the rush as the wave picks me up and carries me toward the beach. I'm not ready to stand on the surfboard yet, but I get up to my knees. A surge of adrenaline pours through me and I lean my head back, feeling the wind whip past.

Lucas is on his feet, turning his surfboard back and forth, his arms out for balance. He whips around and grins at me, his wet hair hanging in his eyes.

God, he's so sexy.

I laugh and wave at him when he jumps down off his board. I managed to stay on mine, and I get back to my tummy so I can paddle toward him.

"That's my girl." He pulls me in and leans down to plant a salty kiss on my lips. "Ready to go again?"

"Yes!"

The sun climbs high in the sky as we catch wave after wave. I laugh and shriek and forget my fear in the face of the exhilaration I feel. By the end of the day, I'm able to get all the way to my feet, although when I try to stand up completely, I still fall over. But it's progress. Lucas and I have so much fun, only the exhaustion of a full day of surfing brings us back to the sandy beach.

He helps me peel off my wetsuit. The beach is deserted, so I take off my swimsuit, intending to change into dry clothes. But Lucas gives me *that look*, and the next thing I know, we're tangled together in the back seat of his car. Sex in a car? Yet another thing I'd never done before I met Lucas.

I was seriously missing out.

He makes me come once with his tongue (he is *so* good at that), and again with his cock. At first, I'm the tiniest bit worried someone will drive by and catch us, but that thought melts away with the feel of his body against mine. He finishes fast, but I have no complaints. His urgency propels me forward, tipping me over into climax in a rush of passion.

Afterward, we get dressed and build a fire. I sit back between his legs, resting against him, while he wraps his arms around me. We warm our hands and feet near the flames, drink a cold beer from the cooler we brought, and cook hot dogs over the fire. The sun dips down toward the ocean, staining the sky purple and orange, and the first stars twinkle overhead.

I can't imagine a more perfect day.

Lucas and I have been dating—for real dating—ever since that morning he broke into my apartment. Although my quest to become end-of-*Grease* Sandy is more or less over, he does still come up with new things for us to do together all the time. We went snowboarding over the winter, which I'd never done before. And I finally faced my fear of zombies and watched a zombie movie with him. I slept at his place that night because I was too scared to go back home, but hey, I watched it.

My parents have finally stopped asking when I'm moving closer to them. Now they've switched to bugging me about coming up to visit more often. But I'll take what I can get. Lucas won them over almost immediately—especially when he started giving my dad investment advice. And my dad only sends me worried texts about half as often as he used to. Although, as soon as he hears I went surfing again, I'm sure he'll send me links to half a dozen articles on water safety. He means well, at least. And I feel good about how things are with them. We've come a long way.

*I've* come a long way.

It's been more than a year since I moved to Jetty Beach, and I've proved to myself that I can make it on my own. I'm learning more every day about how to be in charge of my own life. Sure, I've had Lucas. But he doesn't treat me like I'm helpless or breakable. Seeing myself through his eyes has helped me realize I'm a lot braver than I thought I was.

Although I do still depend on him to kill spiders. I have to draw the line somewhere.

I put my hands in the pockets of my sweatshirt and snuggle in against him. The fire flickers near my feet, keeping my toes warm. He pulls me in tighter, his arms around my waist, and presses his lips against my neck.

"You were awesome out there today," he says.

"Thanks. I had a good teacher."

He laughs a little and kisses my neck again. "Becca?"

"Yeah?"

"Are you happy?"

His question catches me by surprise. Partly because I can't imagine feeling much happier than I do right this minute. And partly because it's so out of the blue.

"I'm *so* happy," I say. "I don't know if you mean right now, or just in general, but the answer is the same both ways."

I feel him nod, but he doesn't say anything else. My heart beats a little faster and a tingle of nervousness runs through my belly. Maybe I'm imagining things, but he seems tense all of a sudden. This reminds me of all the times he showed up at my back door with something planned for me. I feel like he has something up his sleeve.

"Becca?" he says again, the lilt of his voice making my name a question.

"Yeah?"

"I don't want this to end."

I tilt my face up so I can look at him. "I know. It's been such a perfect day."

He brings his lips to mine in a soft kiss. "That's not what I mean."

There's mischief in his eyes and the beginning of a smile tugging at the corners of his mouth. He *is* up to something.

"Stay here for a second, okay?" He gets up and goes to his car.

I wait while he gets in, and when he comes back, he sits cross legged next to me. The fire illuminates his face, flickering against his skin and lighting up his eyes. I shift so I'm facing him, my legs crossed.

He takes a deep breath. "I have something for you. I wasn't sure when I was going to give it to you, but today feels… it feels right."

My breath catches and I stare at him, my eyebrows raised, my lips parted. He can't mean…

He reaches into his sweatshirt pocket and pulls out a small black box. It draws my eyes like a magnet. He looks down at it, turning it with his fingers.

"When we met, I thought I had life all figured out," he

says. "I didn't think I needed anything else. But that was just what I told myself so I wouldn't think too hard about what I was missing. Then you showed up, and I know I'm getting so cheesy here, but you were like a ray of sunshine. I was still broken inside, and little by little, you put me back together."

He pauses and touches my chin, lifting my gaze to meet his.

"I didn't plan on falling in love with you," he says. "I didn't think I was capable of it anymore, to be honest. But Becca, I *adore* you. I love you so much, and when I say I don't want this to end, I mean us. I mean I want you forever."

*I want you forever.*

Tears spring to my eyes and I bite my lower lip. "You do?"

"Yes, I really do." He slowly opens the box, revealing a beautiful diamond solitaire. "Becca, will you marry me?"

I stare at Lucas and a tear breaks free from the corner of my eye to trail down my cheek. It takes me a second to find my voice. I did *not* see this coming.

"Oh, yes." I brush the tear away. "Yes, I will definitely marry you."

He pulls the ring from the box and lifts my left hand. His mouth turns up in a playful smirk and he winks as he slides the ring on my finger. I swear, only Lucas could make putting on an engagement ring feel naughty.

He grabs me, pulling me into his lap, and I wrap my legs around his waist. He kisses me, slow and deep, his arms around me, holding me close. I run my fingers through his hair and taste the salt on our skin. He starts to smile through the kiss, and I can't help but smile too. The next thing I know, we're both laughing so hard we can hardly breathe.

He tips me backward, angling us away from the fire, and

lays me down in the sand. It's cold against my back, but Lucas's warm weight feels so good on top of me. He looks into my eyes for a long moment, then kisses my lips, his mouth soft and gentle.

"I love you, darling," he says. "I'm so glad you're mine."

# AFTERWORD

Dear reader,

Raise your hand if you're ready to move to Jetty Beach!

Yeah, me too. This place, and it's cast of characters, has been so much fun. I definitely have a thing for good but naughty heroes (noticed that yet?), and Jetty Beach seems to be full of them.

When I got to the end of the previous book (Finn and Juliet's story) I was wondering what to do next. I knew I'd feature Lucas, and I knew I'd feature Becca. And then it hit me... the best friends of Finn and Juliet could SO hook up with each other.

But Becca was with Brandon, and that just wouldn't do. I knew from the start that Becca's long term relationship was going to fall apart. Poor thing. She might not have seen it coming, but it was for the best. The first idea I had for this book was actually the opening scene, when Becca gets dumped and pukes on Brandon. I wrote that before I was even sure what the rest of the book was going to be about.

I really liked Becca. She's a little less sassy than some of my other heroines, but I like that she's finally taking a stand for herself. I tried to convey that although she needed Lucas to help her grow, she was standing on her own two feet by the end. Even when she's unexpectedly faced with Brandon, and his new girlfriend, she knows deep down that she can handle it. Having Lucas with her helped, but she wouldn't have fallen apart without him there. That was a cool moment for her.

But my favorite part of this book was Lucas. Specifically, watching Lucas fall in love with Becca, and be so totally oblivious to it. "Gee, I haven't been sleeping around. That's weird." Call it what you want, buddy. From the moment you met her, you were hooked. You just didn't know it.

I loved how he saw Becca for who she was, right from the start. He did help her when she locked her keys in the car, but it wasn't because he wanted to scoop her up and baby her. He was just being neighborly. If she'd been sitting there with her phone in her hand, he would have assumed she could handle it herself.

And I think that's one of the things about their relationship that made it work. He did assume she could do things for herself. He liked pushing her, and making her try things that scared her. But he never for a moment thought that she couldn't get on without him. He saw her as a perfectly capable person, and seeing herself through his eyes helped Becca realize he was right.

Plus, it was utterly adorable to watch him fall for her. By the time they go to her parents' anniversary party, he has it SO BAD for her. He thinks he has everything under control. He has it all worked out. But he's crazy about her.

How can someone be so in love and be so clueless?

Well, he's a GUY, let's be honest about that. Guys are not always super in touch with their emotions. And Lucas inherited (and/or learned) at least some emotional repression from his dad. Plus, Becca didn't blast into his life. His previous experience with love was a lot more tumultuous. Becca was soft and quiet and sweet.

Poor dude never had a chance.

A note about Becca's first surfing experience. That scene is based on something that actually happened to me. I don't usually (as in, never before this) lift personal experiences so directly and put them into a book. But this one just worked, so I went with it. My boyfriend took me surfing in high school and right after I caught my very first wave, he jumped off his board so he could swim over to me, and it flew up and smacked me in the head. I rolled off my board and he had to fish me out (pun intended) and carry me back to the beach. Fortunately, I was not seriously injured—and neither was Becca.

I hope you enjoyed another story in my favorite beach town! And yes, I do know who is next, and yes, it is Gabriel. I know, I know, his story is a long time coming. But rest assured, a book about Gabe is on my writing schedule. And I will do my absolute best to make it worth the wait.

Thanks for reading!
CK

# ALSO BY CLAIRE KINGSLEY

For a full and up-to-date listing of Claire Kingsley books visit www.clairekingsleybooks.com/books/

For comprehensive reading order, visit www.clairekingsleybooks.com/reading-order/

### The Bailey Brothers

Steamy, small-town family series. Five unruly brothers. Epic pranks. A quirky, feuding town. Big HEAs. (Best read in order)

Protecting You (Asher and Grace part 1)

Fighting for Us (Asher and Grace part 2)

Unraveling Him (Evan and Fiona)

Rushing In (Gavin and Skylar)

Chasing Her Fire (Logan and Cara)

Rewriting the Stars (Levi and Annika)

∽

### The Miles Family

Sexy, sweet, funny, and heartfelt family series. Messy family. Epic bromance. Super romantic. (Best read in order)

Broken Miles (Roland and Zoe)

Forbidden Miles (Brynn and Chase)

Reckless Miles (Cooper and Amelia)

Hidden Miles (Leo and Hannah)

Gaining Miles: A Miles Family Novella (Ben and Shannon)

### Dirty Martini Running Club

Sexy, fun stand-alone romantic comedies with huge... hearts.

Everly Dalton's Dating Disasters (Everly, Hazel, and Nora)

Faking Ms. Right (Everly and Shepherd)

Falling for My Enemy (Hazel and Corban)

Marrying Mr. Wrong (Sophie and Cox)

(Nora's book coming soon)

### Bluewater Billionaires

Hot, stand-alone romantic comedies. Lady billionaire BFFs and the badass heroes who love them.

The Mogul and the Muscle (Cameron and Jude)

The Price of Scandal, Wild Open Hearts, and Crazy for Loving You

More Bluewater Billionaire shared-world stand-alone romantic comedies by Lucy Score, Kathryn Nolan, and Pippa Grant

### Bootleg Springs

### by Claire Kingsley and Lucy Score

Hot and hilarious small-town romcom series with a dash of mystery and suspense. (Best read in order)

Whiskey Chaser (Scarlett and Devlin)

Sidecar Crush (Jameson and Leah Mae)

Moonshine Kiss (Bowie and Cassidy)

Bourbon Bliss (June and George)

Gin Fling (Jonah and Shelby)

Highball Rush (Gibson and I can't tell you)

∼

### Book Boyfriends

Hot, stand-alone romcoms that will make you laugh and make you swoon.

Book Boyfriend (Alex and Mia)

Cocky Roommate (Weston and Kendra)

Hot Single Dad (Caleb and Linnea)

∼

**Finding Ivy** (William and Ivy)

A unique contemporary romance with a hint of mystery.

∼

**His Heart** (Sebastian and Brooke)

A poignant and emotionally intense story about grief, loss, and the transcendent power of love.

∼

### The Always Series

Smoking hot, dirty talking bad boys with some angsty intensity.

Always Have (Braxton and Kylie)

Always Will (Selene and Ronan)

Always Ever After (Braxton and Kylie)

**The Jetty Beach Series**

Sexy small-town romance series with swoony heroes, romantic HEAs, and lots of big feels.

Behind His Eyes (Ryan and Nicole)

One Crazy Week (Melissa and Jackson)

Messy Perfect Love (Cody and Clover)

Operation Get Her Back (Hunter and Emma)

Weekend Fling (Finn and Juliet)

Good Girl Next Door (Lucas and Becca)

The Path to You (Gabriel and Sadie)

# ABOUT THE AUTHOR

Claire Kingsley is a #1 Amazon bestselling author of sexy, heartfelt contemporary romance and romantic comedies. She writes sassy, quirky heroines, swoony heroes who love their women hard, panty-melting sexytimes, romantic happily ever afters, and all the big feels.

She can't imagine life without coffee, her Kindle, and the sexy heroes who inhabit her imagination. She lives in the inland Pacific Northwest with her three kids.

www.clairekingsleybooks.com

Printed in Poland
by Amazon Fulfillment
Poland Sp. z o.o., Wrocław